"I swear to you," he promised, "they aren't taking me alive. I'm sorry, Lisa—sorrier than you'll ever know." *And sorrier still for what I haven't told you.*

"Don't. Please." She raised herself onto her toes and brushed the fullness of her warm lips across his. The kiss was soft and fleeting, yet somehow it sent a jolt that blazed through his brain and body as if he'd never experienced a woman's touch before. Desire gripped him, a searing need to turn and claim her mouth in earnest, to find out what it was about her that had somehow stirred that pile of cold ash that was once his beating heart.

"I'll come for you," Cole managed, his voice rough. "And, Lisa, if there's any way—any way at all—to make it happen, I'll be bringing your son with me."

COLLEEN THOMPSON

RELENTLESS PROTECTOR

HARLEQUIN®

entertain, enrich, inspire™

To those who serve and sacrifice…
and the no-less-courageous families who love them.

ISBN-13: 978-0-373-69643-7

Recycling programs for this product may not exist in your area.

RELENTLESS PROTECTOR

www.Harlequin.com

Printed in U.S.A.

ABOUT THE AUTHOR

After beginning her career writing historical romance novels, Colleen Thompson turned to writing the contemporary romantic suspense she loves in 2004. Since then, her work has been honored with a Texas Gold Award, along with nominations for a RITA® Award, a Daphne du Maurier Award and multiple reviewers' choice honors, along with starred reviews from *RT Book Reviews* and *Publishers Weekly*. A former teacher living with her family in the Houston area, Colleen has a passion for reading, hiking and dog rescue. Visit her online at www.colleen-thompson.com.

Books by Colleen Thompson

HARLEQUIN INTRIGUE

CAST OF CHARACTERS

Captain Cole Sawyer—Leaving his elite army ranger unit wasn't easy, but turning his back on a fellow soldier's gorgeous widow in her hour of need is impossible—as impossible as his growing attraction to the courageous young mother who threatens to take his combat-hardened heart by storm.

Lisa Meador—When an ordinary afternoon errand goes terribly wrong, this determined young widow will stop at nothing—including the kidnappers' demands that she commit bank robbery—to free her only child. When a handsome stranger interferes, she enlists his help—never guessing the devastating secret that binds them.

Tyler Meador—Determined to be as brave as his soldier father was in combat, Lisa's five-year-old son relies on his imagination, and his trusty stuffed octopus, to keep his fears at bay.

Lee Ray Hardy—Despite a long rap sheet and a bad drug habit, this career criminal has a soft spot for the kidnapped boy. But will that be enough to save him from his partner's schemes?

Evie LeStrange—A violent sociopath with an ax to grind, Evie wants to get rid of her incriminating encumbrance—but only after inflicting as much pain as possible on a woman she didn't choose at random.

Deputy Trace Sutherland—This by-the-book deputy still loves the ex-wife he's been assigned to ride with, but will either of them survive her reckless disregard for safety?

Deputy Jill Keller—A near-death experience has done little to temper her gung-ho attitude toward law enforcement. But will her lingering love for her ex-husband finally make her see the light?

Prologue

In a grimy motel room somewhere in Oklahoma, a woman picked up a newspaper left behind by the last occupant. No shock there, considering the general state of this dive, but the face staring up at her sent the room whirling around her and nausea squeezing in her stomach.

It was *her,* a brat in her arms, a brave smile on her face. A face the woman in the motel room would know anywhere, no matter how many years had passed. Because she never forgot any of those who had destroyed her.

Most of them, she'd paid back in spades already: the sadistic bitch who'd called herself a mother; the foster father who had raped her, brutally and often; even the juvenile detention officer who'd been such a hard-ass later—every one of them lying in an unmarked grave. But not the one who'd set it all in motion, the one she'd sworn on the memory of all she'd lost to repay—if she could ever find her.

A glance at the photo's caption gave her the bitch's married name, and a line in the article revealed the town where she was living.

The town where she would die—but not before she'd learned what real suffering was all about.

Chapter One

Lisa Meador was running late again, ridiculously late thanks to the passive-aggressive front office manager, who had scheduled her for yet another dental cleaning way too close to school dismissal.

Still in her scrubs following her long afternoon, she was wound up in knots and already thinking about her next errand when she swung into what ought to be the line of parents waiting in cars at her son's elementary school.

Except there was no line. She was the last and only car. The last parent, picking up the last and tiniest of students, who stood with an impatient-looking teacher in attendance.

I'm so sorry, Lisa mouthed before her older-model silver Camry slowed to a complete stop. But the knot of tension in her stomach loosened as five-year-old Tyler came dashing toward the car, his huge smile seeming to run ahead of him.

It was the smile Lisa lived for, the one thing that had kept her breathing, putting one foot before the other, in the thirteen months since her husband, Devin, had been killed by a suicide bomber in Afghanistan.

Only twenty-eight when she was widowed, Lisa was determined not to dwell on the unfairness of her loss. Instead, she focused on the five good years she and Devin had had together and the tawny-haired boy whose antics kept her scrambling to keep up.

The teacher on duty, a plump, graying woman in old-fashioned cat-eyed glasses, did some scrambling of her own to beat tiny Tyler to the back door of Lisa's car and hold it open.

"No running into the circle, Tyler, or you'll have to miss next recess," she warned as the boy clambered into his booster seat like a spider monkey. "We don't want anybody getting hurt, now."

"Yes, ma'am, Mrs. Davies, ma'am." Tyler's back straightened, and his right hand shot stiffly to his brow in his best approximation of a soldierly salute. His dad's salute, remembered only from Skype calls and home videos. Duty done, Tyler snapped the buckle and hugged his plush stuffed octopus in his arms before tacking on a worried "Sorry I forgot again. I'll do better next time."

Mrs. Davies flicked a pointed look toward Lisa before her stern pretense dissolved into a smile. Lisa understood, since it was hard staying angry, even for a minute, at the smallest boy and biggest live wire in the kindergarten class.

"I'll remind him, too," she told the teacher. "And I promise, I'll be here earlier tomorrow."

She swore she would keep that promise, even if it meant a showdown with the most vindictive office manager in all of Coopersville. Because as important as Lisa's job was to her and Tyler's well-being, she refused to give in to the reign of petty evil.

Once they left the school, she turned onto the town's main drag. Her heart constricted as she noticed that most of the businesses had put out both American and Texas flags, along with a host of cheerful signs and banners welcoming home the heroes of the nearby base's returning combat unit.

Devin's combat unit, or what was left of it.

Swallowing back grief, she drew a deep breath and gave a silent prayer of thanks for all those who were coming home to happy families. Walking into their arms instead of being carried in a grim, flag-draped procession.

"I'm really hungry, Mommy," said Tyler. "Can we stop for a kid's meal? Please?"

"Sorry, sweetie," she said, glad for the distraction. "We have to go get Rowdy—the groomer's closing early today. And then we're heading straight home for the good stuff."

Tonight she was determined to cook her son a healthy dinner with some actual vegetables in it, no matter how stressed she was or how tempted by the idea of an easy drive-through pickup.

"But kids' meals *are* the good stuff," he argued. "They have toys inside."

Sighing, Lisa mentally cursed whatever marketing genius had dreamed up putting kiddie kryptonite inside the cartoon-covered boxes. Tyler sulked, refusing her attempts to talk about his school day. Choosing to ignore the behavior, she soon pulled into the parking lot of a small gold bungalow, sliding into a space between a beat-up white panel van and a bright yellow Beetle with a Buttercup's Cuts-4-Pups bumper sticker.

"Come on, champ," Lisa said with as much cheer as she could muster. "Let's go bail out Rowdy. He'll be so glad to see you."

For a moment, Tyler looked as if he meant to balk, but apparently the thought of seeing his beloved dog—a rescue puppy she'd adopted on impulse two days after Devin's funeral—was enough to get him moving.

Five minutes and fifty dollars later, they emerged with

Rowdy, freshly shorn of much of his cream-colored hair. Once he reached the grass, the little dog rolled and peed and jumped and barked and spun like a deranged wind-up toy on the end of his leash. But at least the Lhasa apso mix's excitement had Tyler laughing again.

It had Lisa laughing, too…right up until the moment she felt something hard and unyielding shoved against her lower back.

She didn't know it was a gun at first, not until she heard the hiss of a woman's voice in her ear. "Stay very still, and don't scream. Not unless you want your brat to watch you die."

Lisa's eyes widened, and her muscles froze. Shock waves detonated through her; she couldn't move or breathe or think.

But her eyes instinctively found Tyler, squatting beside Rowdy and rubbing the wriggling animal's belly. Worthless as a watchdog, the animal remained as oblivious as the boy.

"That's such a good girl," the woman praised her, the menace clinging to the words redefining the word "evil" in Lisa's mind forever. "Now get him in the car. We're going for a ride."

Never let an attacker take you to a second location. The advice floated up from memory, one of her police officer dad's grim lessons from her younger years.

"You can have my purse. My paycheck's in it." Her voice trembled. "I'll even sign it for you and give you the PIN for my bank card."

The barrel ground painfully against her backbone. "One bullet in your spine, another in your head. And then I start on him, if you don't follow my directions. *To the letter.*"

"Tyler, honey," Lisa croaked. "Tyler, in the car, please. Take Rowdy with you. Quickly."

Tyler looked up sharply, his blue eyes huge and worried as his gaze moved from her face to whoever was standing behind her. "Hi?" he ventured, his voice very small.

"Better do as your mom says," the stranger advised, and something lurking behind the iced-sugar sweetness of those few words had Tyler scurrying to comply without a word of argument.

As the pressure on her spine eased, Lisa dared to turn her head. Not all the way—she feared she would be shot point-blank if the woman caught her staring—but enough to get a peripheral impression of a taller figure topped with blue-streaked, unnaturally black hair, hacked unevenly to chin length. Dressed in black, too, all skintight straight-leg jeans and a tiny micro T-shirt that clung to small, pigeon's-egg breasts.

"What is it you want?" Lisa asked as the white door of the panel van slid open.

When a skinny man stepped from the opening, fresh dread launched icy daggers through her system. He was slightly taller than the woman. His shaved head and the black chin-strap beard weren't half so alarming as the wild gleam in his eyes and the way sweat plastered his wife-beater T-shirt to a wiry-thin body crawling with dark tattoos.

Could this be about rape, then, if not robbery? Did they mean to take her somewhere in the white van, leaving her child here alone?

Gut-churning as the thought was, Lisa knew that at least Tyler would be safe here. He would run inside the groomer's shop as soon as she disappeared from view. Even if terror froze him in place, someone would soon find him. Then the police would call her sister, who would get here as quickly as she could. Who would raise her child if she had to.

Because Lisa knew if she got inside that white van, she wasn't coming back alive.

"What we want," the woman finally answered, shifting her thin shoulder beneath the strap of the oversize duffel bag slung over it, "is for you to take us all for a little ride in your car. We're going to the main branch of the First National Bank of Coopersville."

Confusion sent Lisa's mind spinning back to thoughts of robbery. "But my bank's the military credit union over on-post."

"You damn well better do what she says!" the man roared, making Lisa jump. "*Exactly,* or it's over."

Hurrying to obey, she fished her keys from her purse, then opened the driver's-side door and got in. Before she could stab the shaking key into the ignition, the woman had climbed into the passenger seat beside her.

More horrifying still was the moment the man climbed into the rear seat, sitting right beside her son, who started wailing loudly.

As Rowdy, on the booster seat's opposite side, began to whine, too, the woman thrust the gun toward Lisa's face. "Shut the brat up, or I swear I'll do it for you."

Panic spiraled through Lisa's body, a sickening physical sensation that took her back to the moment she'd learned of her husband's death. She hadn't been there to stop it, but she wasn't letting this sick couple do anything to her son. Whatever she must endure, she swore she would keep him safe.

With that vow, an eerie, disconnected calm washed over her in warm waves, giving her the strength to turn to Tyler, to reach back and touch his small leg. "Tyler, baby. You have to listen. Listen to me, soldier."

He responded when she called him *soldier,* coming to attention so sharply that she thanked God for this phase he'd been going through for months now. But red blotches stood out on his pale face, and tears trembled on his lashes. If she didn't reach him right away, he would quickly lose it again.

"When Daddy was in battle, he had to keep his troops safe. Rowdy and Octobuddy are your troops now. It's up to you to set a brave example, to keep them safe and calm."

The anxiety in his blue eyes shifted; just like that, he slipped into the plane of childish imagination, a safe haven from this nightmare. "I can... I can be brave," he said uncertainly.

She looked into her only child's face, directing every atom of love and confidence she could muster toward him. "You can be a *hero,* Tyler, with medals just like your dad's and generals coming to salute you. And Daddy will be so proud, watching over you from heaven."

Tyler gave her a crisp salute, his moppet's bangs falling into his eyes. Swallowing past the lump in her throat, Lisa saluted back.

"Real freakin' touching," said the woman, a sneer on her thin face. A face and voice that nudged a memory Lisa couldn't place.

Could she have met this woman before? Inadvertently done something to bring on this horror? Before she could stop herself, the question slipped out. "Who are you?"

To her surprise, the woman's mouth twisted into a cruel smile, and she answered, "You can call me Evie. Let's make it Evie LeStrange. Now give me that damned purse."

As she yanked it away, then pulled a straw bag from her duffel and tossed it at Lisa, the backseat passenger hooted with laughter before the woman sliced her vicious blue gaze his way. He fell silent in an instant, confirming Lisa's suspicion that "Evie" was calling the shots.

Heart pounding, Lisa risked a second question. "Why are you doing this to us? Have I somehow—"

A blur of motion preceded a sharp blow—the barrel of the woman's gun striking the side of Lisa's skull. Her vision dimmed as pain arced through her, but terrified of upsetting Tyler, she did no more than gasp.

Beside her, her assailant snarled, "Any more questions? Good. Now let's get movin'. Bank's closing in a half hour, and trust me, Sweet Girl Baby, you do *not* want to be late."

Sweet Girl Baby. The familiar words sent a queasy ripple through Lisa's midsection, but she was too occupied with keeping herself and her son alive to think about it now.

LONG AND LEAN AND standing tall as Texas, Cole Sawyer strode into First National as if he owned the place. Months of doubt and worry over whether he had done the right thing mustering out of the army had all been vanquished by the letter of acceptance in the inner pocket of his jacket. The letter guaranteeing him a place in the next class of U.S. Marshal recruits two months from now in Georgia.

The army brass had hated losing a warrior in his prime, and his fellow Rangers couldn't understand why a trained sniper, a hawkeyed marksman who could take down a camouflaged enemy a half mile distant, would "bail" on them. Why he would allow a single incident, viewed through his scope, to instantly, irrevocably make him lose his taste for the kind of clean kills that supported his team's mission.

Better he should move his accounts rather than leaving his money at the military credit union, where he would continue running into his former comrades all too often.

Where he would be forced to face their disappointment or, worse yet, their attempts to convince him that in war-time, people died, that he hadn't been the one to kill them.

He was sitting in a glassed-in booth, filling out the paperwork to open his new accounts, when he saw the brunette walking past him toward the teller's counter. After months of self-imposed celibacy, he couldn't help noticing her, his eyes drawn to the curvy figure that her loose raspberry-and-white scrubs could not hide and the wavy, coffee-rich hair that fell well past her shoulders. His gaze flicked to a pretty face, no older than late twenties, and his heart jerked as he was slammed with recognition, followed instantly by guilt.

She was one of the widowed military spouses featured in last month's article in *USA This Morning*—a woman widowed thirteen months before. Widowed because he'd failed her husband.

He'd known that Lisa Meador and her son lived in town still, had made a note of where she worked and found out where their house was, when he was still thinking of going to her and explaining his role in her husband's death. Of begging her forgiveness for that one death, one of many. Somehow, though, his C.O., Drew Woodsen, had gotten wind of it and ordered him to steer clear. Cole would have gone anyway, if Woodsen hadn't made him understand that his appearance would only amount to a selfish—and totally unnecessary—bid for absolution that would end up causing Lisa and her son even more pain.

Cole meant to drag his gaze away before she caught him looking, but there was something in her glazed, wide-eyed stare that brought him to his feet. Something he'd seen frozen on the features of the female terrorist in the moments before she'd self-detonated in the center of that crowded market.

Could Devin Meador's widow be so undone by his death, or facing such financial hardship, that she would actually...

"Is something wrong, Mr. Sawyer?" asked the bank's customer service manager, a stout, middle-aged woman with a sprayed blond helmet of a bob. Following his gaze, she smiled on seeing Lisa. "Oh, she is a pretty thing. A friend of yours?"

"Not yet," he said with a wink he wasn't feeling. "Would it be all right with you if I drop these papers back here first thing in the morning?"

Misreading his distraction, the manager laughed. "Anything for love. You have a pleasant evening."

Cole stepped from her office, feeling for the concealed handgun hidden in his waistband just in case. Licensed to carry in the state of Texas, he had come armed only to safeguard the cashier's check he'd meant to deposit, a check representing the bulk of his life's savings.

Never in his wildest imaginings had he figured on the possibility that he might have to stop a bank job, a holdup by a woman radiating the sort of desperation that got people hurt—or killed.

He hoped his instincts were off, that his own guilt had him imagining things, and the look he'd seen on her face signaled something far more mundane. Maybe she'd been laid off or was behind with a car payment, not planning to resort to a federal crime. As she reached inside an oversize straw handbag at the teller's station, he willed her to come up with a paycheck, or maybe a withdrawal slip or her ID.

He gazed across the bank lobby, but he found no help there. Only a big-bellied, older security guard looking at his watch. Checking to see it was just ten minutes before he could lock the doors and get home to enjoy his evening. Mentally, the man had already clocked out.

And why wouldn't he, with no other customers in the lobby but the fortyish business type filling out his deposit ticket at an island counter and the pretty raspberry-and-white scrubs woman who pulled out a piece of paper and passed it to the teller before shoving her hand back into the bag...?

Where she was holding something, Cole was certain. Something that—damn it all—had to be a gun.

Though he couldn't see the weapon, he knew it from the way the petite, red-haired teller stiffened and took on the same pale green color as the maternity blouse that covered the late-term swell of her midsection. Cole edged a few steps closer, his hand on his own gun.

His heart was thumping, adrenaline priming every nerve and muscle, readying him for a fight he didn't want—the fight to keep everyone inside this bank alive, including his fellow soldier's widow. No matter how justified the circumstances, he knew that any discharge of his weapon would trigger an investigation, which could easily result in his missing the start date for his training class. And heaven only knew when there might be another.

But no matter what it cost him, it wasn't in Cole Sawyer to walk away from trouble, not the sort of trouble that could get a pregnant teller or a distressed widow killed. Swearing he wouldn't fire unless he absolutely had to, he took another cautious step.

"Don't scream, don't even think of triggering an alarm, and you'll be fine, I swear it," Lisa whispered, the tension in her own voice like the sizzling of a fuse.

A fuse quickly burning toward a deadly detonation. Cole saw it all too clearly, as the teller's green eyes widened even farther. She was about to lose it, about to give way to a fit of shrieking guaranteed to spell disaster....

A disaster he had the chance to stop. *A second chance...*

He took another step, trying to gain an angle that wouldn't put the pregnant woman in his line of fire.

He was interrupted by a sharp cry of alarm, not from the teller but from the friendly service manager who'd helped him. "Oh, no!" Her terror echoed off the glass and marble of the room. "He's got a gun!"

She was pointing at *him,* he realized, as Lisa whirled in his direction, her weapon rising from her purse.

Cole acted on instinct, diving to one side to avoid fire from both the robber and the security guard, and getting off a single shot of his own, a shot meant to disable and not kill. Because in spite of all his training and several hard lessons underscoring the damage a wounded combatant could still inflict, an older instinct guided his hand. An instinct prompted by the desperation in the brunette's beautiful brown eyes....

And the trickle of bright red blood already dripping from her hairline before he squeezed the trigger.

Chapter Two

"No!" Lisa shouted without thinking.

At the crack of gunfire, she dropped the unloaded weapon Evie had forced on her and bolted toward the door, her mind consumed with getting to Tyler, who was sitting bravely with his dog and stuffed toy inside the car with a pair of stone-souled criminals.

"You screw this up, it won't go well for him," the self-styled Evie LeStrange had warned her. Lisa had done exactly as they'd ordered, complying to the letter, yet everything was self-destructing all around her.

The next few seconds unfolded in slow motion: the guard reaching for his weapon, then gasping and falling forward, clutching at his chest. For an instant, Lisa thought the tall man who'd fired on her must have somehow hit him. Had the bullet missed her and then ricocheted?

It was only then that she felt the slash of pain across her upper right arm, an injury that explained why she had dropped the gun. But she couldn't think about that now, couldn't think of anything but closing the gap between her and her car before the blue-eyed woman and tattooed man realized—

As her hand shot toward the door, something struck her like a freight train, but it wasn't another bullet. Instead, it was the big, athletic-looking "hero" who'd wrecked everything. She screamed as the speed and force of his tackle slammed her to the floor.

"Please!" Too desperate to register the pain, she struggled to get out from underneath what felt like a brick wall. It was a testament to adrenaline that she partially wriggled free, staring through the glass door—just in time to see her car peeling out.

"My baby! They're taking him," she shouted at the man who'd grabbed her shoulders. "Get off me, you idiot! They'll kill him if I don't bring them the cash."

"WHAT?" COLE's brain felt battered by her words.

"They carjacked us and forced me—please! That's my Camry they're driving off in, and my son is inside. They're getting away."

In a fraction of a second, the pieces spun together: the drip of blood he'd spotted; the sheer terror in her eyes; the medical scrubs, sensible tennis shoes and tired appearance of a woman on her way home from work, not someone planning a crime. And she was frantic to get out of this lobby.

No wonder—*if* she was being truthful. If her son had truly been abducted by carjackers, waiting around for the cops could get him killed.

Another man might have left the matter for the authorities to handle, but if Cole's recent experience as a Ranger had taught him nothing else, it had seared into his brain the lesson that even a moment's hesitation could make the difference between a positive outcome and an unthinkable tragedy. Another Meador family tragedy to add to his account.

The hell with that, he decided, hauling Lisa to her feet. As he dragged her with him out the door, he tuned out everything extraneous, from the bank manager's screams to the businessman's frozen stare to the security guard's slow crumple, his hand still clutching his chest. Most especially Cole ignored the folded letter in his pocket, the future that would mean nothing if he had to allow Devin Meador's child to die to claim it.

"Get into my truck! We'll follow," he shouted as a dark-skinned man in work coveralls ducked behind a vehicle.

The panicked reaction made Cole realize he was still carrying his Glock in plain sight. But he didn't give a damn about that; this moment was combat, plain and simple, one thing he understood. *Act first and deal with cleanup when the smoke clears.* They had to catch up with her car, which had taken a right out of the lot, then zoomed past a strip mall before careening around a curve and disappearing.

Desperate as Lisa Meador was, she still hesitated for an instant, clearly paralyzed by her fear of the man who had just shot and jumped her.

"It's all right!" he shouted at her. "Get in. I'm Ranger Captain Cole Sawyer."

Whether it was his rank, the mystique of the Ranger reputation or desperation to reach her son, she scrambled into his truck, a big black Ram that should eat up the distance between them and her sedan in no time. When he fired up the engine, he saw that he was leaving prints all over, bloody prints from where he'd fought to hold her down.

"That way." She pointed out the direction the silver car had taken. "I'll bet they're heading out of town on Sunset."

He zoomed through a narrow gap in the light traffic, setting off the squeal of wheels as he bulled his way in. He focused on a wreck just ahead, where a motorcycle lay on its side, its leather-clad rider climbing free. He took it as a sign that the fleeing car had made the left, most likely cutting off the cyclist.

Forced to slow to avoid hitting another driver who had stopped to help the downed rider, he turned onto Sunset Avenue, toward the tree-lined river, a perfect spot to dump a small corpse. He tried to wipe the thought from his mind, to remind himself of a recent news story about a Dallas carjacker who, after discovering a sleeping toddler in a backseat, had carefully dropped off the sleeping child in her car seat outside a fire station, where she was soon found safe. Maybe there was hope these criminals would have mercy on Lisa's son, too.

But there were no safe havens along the muddy Brazos River, nothing but the rough dirt roads traveled by fishermen and boaters, or, more often, by hungry coyotes and scavenging feral hogs. So even if the boy did get dropped off somewhere alive, he and Lisa had damned well better find him quickly, before they lost the light.

As Cole zoomed toward the outskirts of town, small businesses gave way to well-kept older houses, many with equally well-kept gardens or pens containing a few horses or some kid's 4-H heifer. After all the violence he'd seen in the Middle East, it was stunning to think of crimes as serious as robbery and abduction affecting this seemingly idyllic place.

"Tyler, baby, hold on," Lisa murmured. "Mama's coming."

Noting her pallor, he suspected she was closing in on shock. "There's a clean hand towel in the glove box," he said. "You'll need to put pressure on that arm to slow the bleeding."

Not seeming to hear him, she kept staring out the windshield. "We'd just picked up our dog at the groomer's when she shoved a gun in my back. Then she made me take her and her partner in my car."

Making note that one of her assailants had been female, he repeated his suggestion as an order. "Get the towel out *now*. Apply pressure, or you'll pass out. Then where will your son be?"

"You know what, *Captain?*" she fired back. "If you hadn't gone and interfered, this would already be over."

"Maybe you didn't notice, but that teller you were terrorizing was about to scream when I made my move. You think I was going to stand there and let an armed robber shoot a pregnant woman? Or *me?*"

"If you'd just stayed out of it—"

"Are you going to sit there arguing until you keel over, or are you going to listen and help me save your kid?"

Her wide-eyed gaze flicked toward him, but after a moment's hesitation, she did as he'd ordered, then returned her attention to the road.

"Buckle up." Shoving his gun beneath the seat, he followed his own advice. There was every indication this was going to be a bumpy ride.

The click of her seat belt assured him she was holding herself together for her child's sake. Probably wasn't even feeling any pain.

But as obvious as her distress was, he reminded himself that, widow or not, she might not be the innocent she'd claimed to be. For all he knew, she could be a willing conspirator, one who didn't trust her partners not to dispose of the encumbrance of her child now that their scheme had gone to hell. If she had really been so irresponsible as to willingly leave the boy in the getaway car while she'd knocked off a bank, she was a far cry from the caring mother the newspaper article had made her out to be.

Unthinkable as it sounded, he couldn't rule out the

possibility. Which meant that for the moment he couldn't fully trust anything she said.

"What's really going on here, Lisa Meador?" he asked, knowing that, even under duress, the use of a person's name was the one thing most likely to gain his or her attention. Or cooperation, which was critical right now.

"How do you know my name?" she asked.

"I saw that article in the newspaper," he said, though he'd known who she was long before that. "Your son's name is Tyler, isn't it?"

Tears leaking, she nodded. "He's only five, and he looked so scared and little in his car seat. How can they do this to him, after everything we've been through?"

Compassion squeezed in his chest. So much for keeping his head and reserving judgment. If her son wasn't really in that car with two kidnappers, she had to be the best liar on the planet. Or a truly gifted actress who knew exactly how to push his buttons.

Changing the subject, he said, "We need to call the sheriff's office. Bring them in on the chase."

The moment the words were out, a stomach-dropping realization hit him. Of all the damned luck. "Ah, hell. I don't have my cell phone."

Since mustering out three weeks earlier, he'd gotten back into the habit of never leaving home without it. Unfortunately, his habit of checking his pockets before doing laundry hadn't been as quick to return. He'd cursed himself this morning, then ordered a replacement, which his provider had promised would be expressed to him tomorrow. Hell of a lot of good that did him now. "What about you, Lisa? You have a phone?"

"That woman took it when she switched my purse with this bag. Then she hit my head with her gun right in front of Tyler. I was so scared he would cry again and the man with the tattoos would..." Her voice choked down to nothing.

So she'd been pistol-whipped as well as shot, in addition to the emotional trauma they'd inflicted. *Allegedly* inflicted, he reminded himself, though his conscience screamed that he owed it to her to believe her. Owed it to her to make things right, though he'd been forbidden to make contact with her.

He drilled her with another question. "Tell me more about these people. Did you know either one?"

"Not the skinny man with all the tattoos, I'm sure of that. But the woman—" She pointed with the bloody towel. "Look. Is that a car?"

It had to be. Beyond a ridge of trees, a rising yellowish dust cloud indicated a vehicle traveling a rutted access road running alongside the muddy Brazos River, no more than a mile or so ahead and to their right. It was heading toward them, but the timing convinced him it had to be their quarry. Maybe they'd dumped her son, then turned around to head back to the main road and make their escape.

Or maybe all that was just a fantasy borne of his desperate hope that this rash act would quickly pay off. That he hadn't just thrown away his future for a beautiful pair of lying brown eyes.

Chapter Three

As the truck jounced along the narrow, tree-lined dirt road, agony flared in Lisa's head and right arm with every bump. Swallowing back a cry of pain, she gritted her teeth and braced herself. She had to get through these next few minutes, had to put her injuries out of her mind until she had her son safely in her arms.

She focused on that image, on Tyler's smile beaming and Rowdy's tail wagging beside him. She poured her soul into a prayer that the vicious Evie and her partner would drop him off and keep going. That all they'd really wanted was the money and not revenge against a helpless child.

"Hurry," she urged Cole Sawyer, her senses so abnormally heightened that she cataloged every detail of the man she had no choice but to depend on. The strong hands on the wheel, the jaw set with determination, the steel-eyed gaze peering out the windshield—everything about him radiated power and the confidence of a man in his prime. As she would expect from a Ranger, his light brown hair was cut military-short, and now it flashed, tipped with gold, as he drove through long, low rays of sunlight splintered by the trees.

He might be helping her now, but she could not forget what his interference might have cost her. Couldn't let go of her fury until her only child—everything that she had left of Devin—was recovered safe and sound.

The truck jolted through a washed-out dip, and black splotches splashed across her vision. Unable to will away the pain shooting through her head and body, she cried out as a wave of dizziness engulfed her.

"Hold on, Lisa," he urged. "We'll be on them any second."

Groaning, she slumped against the door, her gaze drifting, drooping, until Cole said, "See? They're coming this way. Tell me, is it them?"

It was like a hip-deep slog through hardening concrete, sucking in a deep breath and forcing herself to sit up. Finding the bloodstained towel and pressing it against her oozing wound, she welcomed the stab of agony to rouse her.

But it was the sight of the gun in Cole's hand that brought her fully to awareness, that and the dark resolve in those flint-gray eyes of his. He meant to shoot the two abductors if he had to. But what about Tyler? He could be hit, maybe even killed, in the cross fire.

Fresh adrenaline surging through her, she focused on the bumper of the vehicle emerging from the trees. She clamped down on her terror and tuned out the roaring in her head.

"No!" she cried. "That isn't my car."

Her denial didn't stop Cole from pulling into the center of the dirt road and blocking the beat-up sedan coming their way.

As the gun disappeared beneath his jacket, he ordered, "Stay here, and I'll find out if this guy knows anything."

"No. I'm coming, too. I have to…" Lisa began, until the trees, the truck, the entire world, spun like a whirlwind all around her. Before she could say more, the black splotches roared back with a vengeance, and she slumped a second time and went completely limp.

Cole grimaced when he saw her pass out, though it solved one potential problem. If the other driver got one look at the blood on her, there could be a lot more trouble than either he or Lisa needed.

Climbing from his Ram, he waved his hands urgently, trying his best to look like someone in distress rather than a threat. The shaggy-bearded, graying driver in faded overalls stared at him, his expression a mixture of caution and confusion. Cole could not be certain, but he thought he saw the man reach for something underneath his seat.

Possibly a weapon, and Cole didn't blame him, not in this secluded, rural spot. He approached slowly, keeping his palms raised.

The window lowered, and a wary squint creased the corners of the driver's eyes. "You need help, mister? You hurt?"

He was staring at the smear of blood on Cole's hand. Damn it. Cole had to come up with something quick to get the driver on his side with a minimum of explanation—and no suspicious-sounding details about a bank robbery gone wrong.

Improvising, he said, "I was coming home from work, and saw these two thugs, a man and woman, robbing my wife right in our driveway. Before I could stop them, they hit Lisa and took off in our Camry with our five-year-old inside."

The fisherman paled, barely managing a low "Damn, mister."

"We followed them to Sunset Avenue before they got away," Cole said. "But when I saw the dust coming off this road, I thought—did you see them? Did they pass you? We have to get our Tyler back before they—"

"No, sorry. That was only me, comin' up to grab the tackle box I forgot. No car could go any fu'ther back. There's a big tree 'cross the road, and no way past but over."

Cole cursed softly, his heart sinking at this failure. A mistake that might cost Lisa Meador's child his life. "Damn, I've just given them an even bigger lead. I've gotta get back after them on Sunset."

"You report this to the sheriff?"

"No time." He shook his head, the knot in his gut tightening. "We have to hurry."

"Wait! We need to call 9-1-1 and get you some backup. And what about your wife? Is she hurt?"

But Cole was already sprinting back to his truck. Leaping inside, he jammed it into gear and made a sloppy three-point turn, taking out a couple of small trees with his bumper. By that time he was past caring about any dents and scratches, or whether or not the fisherman actually called for help. Waiting for a patrol car would take too long and result in hours of interviews. He had to get back on the road and catch up with the Camry fast.

Reaching the end of the dirt track, he waited for traffic. "Come on, come on," he said, foot tapping. As the clutter of vehicles passed, however, another glance at the unconscious woman stopped him from pulling out again.

A few more drops of blood had dripped down her temple, a startling contrast against her pallor. Full and parted, her lips had gone as colorless as a corpse's. Which meant that her injuries might be more serious than he'd thought.

As badly as he needed to get going, he was seized with the fear that his bullet might have killed her just as surely as his failure had cost her husband his life. Throwing the truck into Park, he felt for the carotid pulse beside her windpipe, a practiced move he had repeated on many a military mission.

His pounding heart pushed into his throat, but this time, thank God, he was not checking a dead body. He felt the flutter of her pulse, more rapid than it should be, but she was alive. Determined to keep her that way, Cole found a first-aid kit he kept beneath the seat, along with a clean T-shirt he had stuffed inside the bag he'd planned to take to the gym later. Thankful for the basic combat medic training the Rangers had provided, he got out and went around to her side, then ripped the shirt at the seams and improvised a pressure bandage for her arm.

Every second delayed what he now saw as his mission, so he worked with swift efficiency, thankful to be finished before the fisherman showed up with more questions to delay them.

He snatched up an old army blanket from behind the front seat, then tossed it over Lisa to help protect her from shock. After slamming the door behind him, he made his way behind the wheel.

Strapping in, he pushed the pickup's powerful V-8 to eat up the lost miles and within minutes overtook the knot of traffic that had delayed him. He deftly passed one vehicle after another until a blind curve obscured his vision and he was forced to flash his high beams at the clueless driver of an ancient rust bucket puttering at the head of the parade. When the car still failed to yield, he tapped the horn twice until the old woman finally pulled onto the shoulder.

After that the road unspooled before him in a dark, unbroken ribbon. He goosed the gas again, quickly gaining speed. But what if he was wrong, if right at the outset he'd guessed incorrectly that the kidnappers were heading out of town on this rural farm-to-market road? And what about the intersection he knew was coming up? Though they might well keep to the smaller roads in the hope of avoiding capture, that would be slower than the interstate.

Each option had its advantages and pitfalls, so how was he to choose the right one? And how could he be certain he wasn't chasing after a mirage, a desperate wish to find redemption for the unforgivable?

LISA FOUGHT HER WAY through the blackness, through her pain, and toward the son who needed her.

"Tyler," she murmured, forcing her eyes open, blinking at the way the landscape had shifted into grassy hills studded with occasional rocky outcrops.

All too quickly, memory roared back and she choked down a cry. Bolting upright, she looked toward the man who might have cost her everything.

"Where's my son?" she asked helplessly. "What happened?"

"He wasn't down that dirt road." A grimace tightened Cole's square jaw. "They didn't go that way."

"You're sure?"

"Sure as I can be about anything right now." He flicked an assessing look in her direction. "You feeling any better?"

A laugh slipped out, dry and mirthless. "You really don't want to know the answer to that question."

"There's some aspirin in the first-aid kit if you can reach it."

Though her head pounded with the movement, she picked up the plastic box off the floorboard, mostly relying on her uninjured left arm. She found the bottle but couldn't open it one-handed.

Passing it to him, she asked, "Could you, please?"

CAST OF CHARACTERS

Captain Cole Sawyer—Leaving his elite army ranger unit wasn't easy, but turning his back on a fellow soldier's gorgeous widow in her hour of need is impossible—as impossible as his growing attraction to the courageous young mother who threatens to take his combat-hardened heart by storm.

Lisa Meador—When an ordinary afternoon errand goes terribly wrong, this determined young widow will stop at nothing—including the kidnappers' demands that she commit bank robbery—to free her only child. When a handsome stranger interferes, she enlists his help—never guessing the devastating secret that binds them.

Tyler Meador—Determined to be as brave as his soldier father was in combat, Lisa's five-year-old son relies on his imagination, and his trusty stuffed octopus, to keep his fears at bay.

Lee Ray Hardy—Despite a long rap sheet and a bad drug habit, this career criminal has a soft spot for the kidnapped boy. But will that be enough to save him from his partner's schemes?

Evie LeStrange—A violent sociopath with an ax to grind, Evie wants to get rid of her incriminating encumbrance—but only after inflicting as much pain as possible on a woman she didn't choose at random.

Deputy Trace Sutherland—This by-the-book deputy still loves the ex-wife he's been assigned to ride with, but will either of them survive her reckless disregard for safety?

Deputy Jill Keller—A near-death experience has done little to temper her gung-ho attitude toward law enforcement. But will her lingering love for her ex-husband finally make her see the light?

ABOUT THE AUTHOR

After beginning her career writing historical romance novels, Colleen Thompson turned to writing the contemporary romantic suspense she loves in 2004. Since then, her work has been honored with a Texas Gold Award, along with nominations for a RITA® Award, a Daphne du Maurier Award and multiple reviewers' choice honors, along with starred reviews from *RT Book Reviews* and *Publishers Weekly*. A former teacher living with her family in the Houston area, Colleen has a passion for reading, hiking and dog rescue. Visit her online at www.colleen-thompson.com.

Books by Colleen Thompson

HARLEQUIN INTRIGUE
1286—CAPTURING THE COMMANDO
1302—PHANTOM OF THE FRENCH QUARTER
1376— RELENTLESS PROTECTOR

He popped the top and handed back the open container. "Take that water from the center console. It's not the freshest, but you need to drink as much of it as you can. It'll help keep you from blacking out again."

She forced herself to wash down two of the tablets, then finish every drop of the water.

"Thanks," she managed, struggling to stave off the panic flashing through her brain like summer lightning.

"We're coming up on an intersection with the interstate in just a couple miles. I'm figuring they'll stick to back roads, since for all they know, there's already an AMBER Alert out for your son. What do you think?"

Anxiety paralyzed her. Maybe they should make finding a phone a priority so the police could really activate the alert. But she couldn't bear the thought of losing their chance to catch up with Tyler. If only she had some way of knowing which route the kidnappers might have taken.

A single thought pierced the fog: the final errand on her day's list. "They'll have to stop for gas soon. I was going to fill up on my way home from the groomer's."

"If they cut over to the interstate, there'll be an exit in about ten miles if they backtrack or another twenty-five or so if they keep heading west."

"If they stay on this road, there's a little town up ahead." She'd driven through it last month, on the way to a friend's ranch, where Tyler had taken his first horseback ride. The memory of his laughter choked her, but she swallowed hard and forced herself to focus. "There's a mom-and-pop store on the main drag—look, you see the sign?"

"Be pretty hard to miss that," Cole said.

Large and crudely painted, the homemade billboard stood along the grassy roadside. *Texas Two-Step, Gas-Groceries-Grill, 8 Miles Ahead, Y'all Come See Us!*

Not far ahead, she saw a more official sign, with its

arrow pointing to the right, indicating a connection to the interstate. And the knowledge crashed down on her that if she made the wrong choice, Tyler could be as lost to her as the husband she had buried.

AMPED UP ON THE candy bars she seemed to live on, his lover drove in a dangerous, lock-jawed silence that even Lee Ray Hardy was afraid to interrupt. He didn't kid himself that "Evie," as she'd demanded he keep calling her, did much more than tolerate him at the best of times, but the drugs were great, the sex mind-blowing and he found her fascinating, like a glittery-scaled cobra that might strike at any moment.

Might strike him dead, he dimly realized, but he was powerless to pull away. Especially as long as she kept him supplied with the crystal meth that had consumed whatever chance he'd ever had at an ordinary life.

Beside him, the boy's eyelids drooped, thanks to the cold medicine Evie had used to spike the juice box from her duffel. Fighting sleep, he studied Lee Ray's inked arms until his face screwed up with disapproval. "Teacher says you're not s'posed to let people draw on your skin," he said sleepily. "She says you can get in real big trouble for it. With the principal."

In spite of himself Lee Ray grinned. "Yeah, well, there's not much any principal can do to me that ain't been done already," he said. "Besides, these're the kind of pictures that don't come off."

"Not even with soap?"

"Already tried that," Lee Ray joked, though he couldn't recall the last time he'd had a bath or shower. It was one of those things he never thought of on his own, but Evie always made him before sex. Not that there'd been much of that since she'd grown so obsessed with tracking down the woman whose photo she'd spotted in some newspaper story.

"So you have to keep them always?" the boy asked. A cute kid, Lee Ray had to admit, with those drowsy blue eyes peering up from beneath the shaggy blond-brown bangs. And except for a rash of tears after Evie had ordered Lee Ray to get rid of that snarling, snapping little mutt of his, the boy had barely cried.

"Always," Lee Ray answered him. "Don't you like my tats, dude?"

Though he held on to the stuffed octopus for dear life, the kid peered at his arm and neck critically, then pointed at the scowling pirate on his left arm. "I like that one, sort of. Except he looks a little scary. You got any cartoons?"

There was one cartoonish naked lady splayed obscenely across his chest, but Lee Ray shook his head instead of lifting his shirt.

"No cartoons," he said, "but you see this?" He showed off what once had been a decent biceps. "This one here's an eagle."

"Shut the hell up back there, will you? You're givin' me a mother of a headache, all that yackin'." Evie's warning sliced him, sharper than the look in her violently blue eyes.

It was a reminder, too, that he had no business getting attached to any rug rat. Especially not one his volatile girlfriend had planned on taking from the start.

He had no idea what she meant to do with the kid, since she'd never seen fit to clue him in on her plans. But whatever it was, he thought as dread tightened his gut, it was bound to be a lot worse than what had happened to the dog.

Chapter Four

The first of several officers on the scene, Deputy Trace Sutherland had never seen a damned thing like this in his sixteen years with the Tuller County Sheriff's Department. Sure, the area had its share of property crimes and assaults, even the rare murder, but a bank holdup in broad daylight, with a hostage taken?

All around him, witnesses continued jabbering, from bank employees to the only other customer who'd been here, to another man who'd seen an armed assailant force a dark-haired woman into his truck.

"He acted like he just wanted to ask that poor girl for a date or something," the customer service manager repeated as she twisted a wad of tissue into pieces. Her eyes wide and wet, she added, "I warned everyone when I saw him going for his gun. He *claimed* his name was Cole, Cole Sawyer, and that he'd recently left the army."

"Probably needed money," the witness from the parking lot interjected. "Lot of them veterans're having trouble finding work."

As the group rattled on, basically rehashing the few facts they had already given, a feminine cry interrupted from across the lobby. Excusing himself, Trace made a beeline to where the EMTs were helping the very shaken, very pregnant teller, who lay curled with her hands clutching her abdomen and her face screwed up in a grimace.

"Her water broke. We'd better get her on the ambulance," said one of the EMTs as she and her partner raised the gurney.

"That's fine," Trace said, then looked down at the young teller, his expression softening at the terror in her eyes. "You just worry about yourself and that baby right now, Mrs. Rowan. We'll send somebody to interview you about the incident once you're feeling better."

At least they would be able to question her later. The security guard, already en route to the hospital after three shocks had failed to restore a normal cardiac rhythm, wouldn't likely survive.

If he did die, or if, God forbid, the teller lost her baby, their suspect would face charges of murder in addition to attempted armed robbery and abduction. Which meant they'd better damned well find the culprit fast.

Trace's boss, the rotund but always-competent Sheriff Stewart, hurried over, pulling his phone from his ear. "We've got a report, some kinda chase situation out on Sunset. Suspect's black Ram pickup appeared to be pursuing an older silver Camry as it fled the scene of a motorcycle wreck. Accomplice, maybe? Anyway, you take Jill and head out that way. I'll have the dispatcher contact you with more info as it comes in."

"Take my—take Jill?" Trace's stomach dropped as his gaze cut toward the tall, uniformed woman now sorting out the witnesses, her sleek wheat-colored ponytail hanging halfway down her back. *Not her. Not now.* He wasn't ready for this. What was she even doing working his shift today?

"Yeah. Her unit's in the shop, and all our reserve cars—

you know our budget issues. She's been playing chauffeur for me today, but I can drive myself."

"Yes, sir," Trace said, because it was the only possible answer. He wasn't about to hold up something this urgent simply because he dreaded riding with his ex-wife. They were both professionals, so they could suck it up and do their duty.

"We'll see if we can track down this Sawyer fella's plates and put out a BOLO on him," the sheriff said.

"That'd be great." A "Be On the Lookout" alert to all surrounding counties could easily result in a quick capture—and less time on the road with a woman who despised him.

A woman he would do anything to go back in time with to undo his mistakes.

"WHAT IF I picked wrong?" Lisa asked Cole for the third time as they sped toward the tiny town of Coffee Creek.

He had no idea how to answer, since all the what-ifs were eating him alive, too. That, and the undeniable fact that dusk was staking its claim. If they didn't catch a break by nightfall...

"No more," he said firmly. "We both agreed they'd be more worried about getting caught on the interstate than making time."

She took a deep breath, clearly making an effort to pull herself together. He had admire how well she succeeded, how even under these horrific circumstances she was able to push past pain and panic, and do what needed to be done.

"We should stop in town. Ask around to see if anyone has seen them," she suggested, looking stronger than she had looked earlier. Stronger than any woman should ever have to be.

He nodded his agreement. "We ought to fuel up any-way, pick up a couple things in case we're on the road longer than we think."

She hesitated before erupting. "I can't stand this wor-rying and wondering if every tiny decision is the wrong one. If I should have stayed and talked to the authorities instead of dragging you out here, running off in what might be the wrong— Stop, Cole! Pull over here, quick."

He looked where she was staring, into the unmown ditch in front of a fenced pastureland dotted with live oaks. Something was moving down there, too low for him to see.

As he skidded to a stop some thirty feet beyond it, he prayed he wasn't seeing what he was afraid of. That the abductors hadn't tossed a living child from a speeding car. He threw the truck in gear and bailed out, intent on beat-ing Lisa to what might be a horrific sight, his instincts demanding that he protect her from it.

Despite her injuries, she was out of the truck and run-ning before he was, calling, "Come on, sweetie! It's okay. Come to Mama!"

She dropped to her knees as a little blond dog emerged from the tall grasses, yelping and wagging furiously as he limped toward her on three legs.

"It's Rowdy," Lisa cried, trying to fend off the animal's frantic kisses. "They must have dumped him out here. Do you know what that means? We've been driving in the right direction after all."

But as reassuring as that thought was, Cole was already running along the roadside, looking for any sign that the abductors, in their haste to rid themselves of their bur-dens, might have dumped a child, too.

Lisa quickly caught on, staggering after him and shout-ing, "Tyler! Tyler! I'm here!"

There was no reply, only the whisper of an evening breeze through the grasses and the screech of a red-tailed hawk in the distance.

They searched frantically, kicking through weeds and climbing down into the ditch, stopping periodically to call again, then listen. They found no sign of Tyler, not a toy or shoe or shirt. And not, thank heaven, his small corpse, which made Cole wonder if the boy's abductors had decided they wanted to hang on to him for some reason. Maybe to hold him for ransom, or as a hostage in case they were caught, or, God forbid, for some darker purpose. One tiny, optimistic corner of Cole's psyche held out a dim hope that maybe the female captor had buried maternal instincts and planned to keep Tyler for herself. Then, at least, he would remain safe long enough to be found.

A few yards distant, Lisa abruptly stiffened, then looked down at her dog. "Where's Tyler, Rowdy?" she asked, her strained voice pitching higher. "Where is he? Where's Tyler? Hide-and-seek, boy."

The little dog's ears pricked up, and he spun in circles barking. When she tried a second time, he did the same.

She shook her head, her face moon-pale with strain. And dangerously appealing, with the breeze ruffling the soft waves that framed it. Waves bronzed by the slanting gold rays of a dying Texas sun. "It's no use. Tyler isn't here, Cole. If he were, Rowdy would take us to him. If I'd been halfway thinking, I would have tried that stupid game the second we found Rowdy."

"Well, I'm glad you did think of it, no matter when." *And gladder still he didn't lead us to a body.* "Now we can get to the gas station and find out if someone saw where they went. Then we'll call the authorities so they can get an AMBER Alert going and apply some real manpower to getting your son back safely."

It would also be smart, he knew, to explain what had happened and maybe extricate himself before she found out what his connection to her was. And if he got out in a timely manner, maybe there was some chance of coming through this without totally derailing the career change he had already given up the best friends he would ever have in this lifetime, along with his retired army colonel father's respect, to pursue.

As they reached the passenger side of his truck, Lisa skewered him with a look. "Of course I want the AMBER Alert. But you're thinking about stopping, aren't you? About getting out of this mess and leaving Tyler out there somewhere."

He was stunned by her perceptiveness, or was he just that transparent? "It might be in your son's best interest if we handed this over to the professionals."

"You mean in *your* best interest, don't you?" A fierce light blazed in her brown eyes. "You'll get to walk away from all this, go back to your cozy house and have a beer or hang out with your girlfriend and forget it. But I wonder, will you tell her how you were the one who started shooting and got my child kidnapped? The one who shot a woman with nothing but an unloaded weapon in her hand?"

Her accusations kicked his conscience, but they were far from the whole story. "First off, there's no girlfriend and not enough beer in the damned world to forget this. And how the hell was I to know that gun in your hand wasn't loaded? If you have to blame somebody, you might as well blame yourself for pointing it at me."

"You startled me—or that woman at the bank did, yelling about you going for a weapon. I never meant to point the gun. Never wanted to hurt anyone or do anything but get out of that bank and buy my child's freedom."

Cole blew out a deep breath, forcing himself to consider the possibility that despite her tears and the fact that the dog had clearly been dumped, she could still be lying. Over the course of his career, some of the most impassioned pleas and speeches he'd ever heard were given by skilled deceivers out to manipulate the listener's emotions. Out to exploit another person's basic decency to achieve their selfish goals.

Maybe years of wartime service had hardened him, making him too cynical, too guarded, to allow himself to feel. Or maybe he wanted to believe that she was somehow involved because it was easier than dealing with his own debt to her family.

"Do you want to stand here arguing until we lose the light, or would you rather do something to help your kid?" Angry with both himself and the situation, he heard his voice coming out far harsher than he meant it to. Trying to make up for this, he opened the door for her, then scooped up the little dog, who limped behind as it kept one front paw raised. Gently, he deposited the trembling animal on the floorboard, sparing a moment to stroke its head to reassure it that he meant no harm.

Looking back to Lisa, he asked, "How 'bout you let me give you a hand up, too?"

He thought she would argue, refusing his offer out of spite. Instead, she sighed and nodded, clearly realizing how tough it would be to climb up into the cab without aggravating her injured arm.

He moved in close behind her. Too close, because the scent of her, or of whatever sweet vanilla shampoo she'd used, touched off an attraction as instinctive as it was unthinkable. But he smelled the blood on her, as well, a sharp reminder that their situation was deadly serious.

After boosting her up to the seat, he ran around the truck and jumped inside.

As he started toward town again, he registered the fact that Lisa had bent over in her seat. Just as he was about to ask what she was doing, she shoved aside her straw bag and then sat up and showed him a spiky, ball-like seed between her fingers.

"Just a burr between his paw pads," she said, nodding toward the dog. "Otherwise, he seems fine."

Within minutes they rolled into the tiny town of Coffee Creek. What must have once been a small but thriving little farm and ranch supply stop had withered to a collection of boarded brick and peeling wooden buildings. Even the tiny post office had been closed, he noticed, but the lone holdout, the Texas Two-Step, had a handful of pickups and a peeling old sedan parked out front. There was no sign of her Camry, but he hadn't figured the abductors would waste any more time here than they had to.

He pulled up to one of the fuel pumps and told Lisa, "I'll start pumping and then go inside to ask questions. I want you to stay—"

"You've got to be kidding," she said as she got out, carrying the straw handbag. Pausing just a moment, she gave the dog a pat. "Stay, Rowdy. I'll be right back."

Cole hurried after her. "You're pretty bloody," he warned. "You might alarm whoever's—"

"Two crazy criminals took my son," she snapped as she strode toward the low brown building. "Do you really think I give a damn whose appetite gets spoiled?"

The door jingled as she pushed it open and charged inside, as bold as any Ranger. And Cole could only pray that in her state of mind she wouldn't start a panic—and that word had not preceded their arrival of a desperate bank robber and his female accomplice on the run.

Chapter Five

In spite of the bell that announced her entrance, none of the half dozen people gathered near the counter turned a head to look Lisa's way when she walked in. Instead, they were clearly transfixed by a wildly gesticulating, red-faced man with his back to her.

"Then I watched that scrawny, tattooed bastard make off with my Explorer, right out of this lot. Where the hell's that deputy?"

An attractive brunette in a blue smock gestured for calm. "Now, take it easy, Clem. I just got off the phone with the sheriff's office. They'll have someone out in no time at—"

"Which way was he driving?" Lisa interrupted. "And did you see an older silver Camry with a woman and my little boy inside?"

Every head snapped toward her, horror written in their faces as they took in her blood-spattered shirt and bandaged arm.

"Please," she begged the owner of the stolen SUV, "you have to help me. They carjacked me in Coopersville and took off with my son inside the Camry. He's only five years old."

"You poor thing," said the brunette, whose name tag

read *Karla*. "You're hurt, darling. Let me call an ambulance—"

"There's no time. I'll be fine." Though pain hovered in the background, Lisa barely registered it.

"We've been trailing them in my truck," said Cole, who had come in behind her. "I'm Captain Cole Sawyer, Army Ranger, and I witnessed the abduction."

The firm authority in his voice demanded both respect and cooperation as he added, "We'll need a plate number, and a good description of the vehicle and where it was heading, a few supplies and a quick fill-up so we can try to catch them."

Clem was the first to recover from his shock. "You'll find my Explorer?"

"The boy's our first priority," Cole answered, "but I'll do what I can."

A man with a bushy gray mustache and a cowboy hat quickly nodded. "I served our country, too, sir. Let me get you started with that fill-up."

As he hurried off, Karla took charge, asking Cole and Lisa, "You notify the Tuller County Sheriff?"

"The kidnappers took my purse and phone," Lisa said.

Cole shook his head, his mouth tightening. "And I didn't have one on me."

The waitress nodded. "Tell me, what do you need?"

In record time, Karla, who was apparently the owner, directed her customers to help gather up first-aid supplies, drinks, food and assorted other items they deemed helpful, while the owner of the stolen Explorer described his four-year-old blue SUV.

Once they were ready, Cole tried to press a handful of twenties on Karla, but she waved him off.

"Forget it." Her compassionate blue eyes found Lisa's, and she pulled something from her pocket and pressed it into Lisa's hand. "Just get out there and find your little boy."

It was a cell phone.

"Reception's pretty spotty out here, but you'll find places you can use it. I've got another phone here." Karla jerked her chin to indicate a corded model on the counter. "I'll look up the Tuller County Sheriff's number and let them know what you've told us."

"Please tell them about my son," said Lisa. "If you have something to write on, I'll give you his name and my Camry's plate number so they can put out an AMBER Alert right away."

"Of course." Karla hurried to get her a pen and order pad.

"Thank you so much." Lisa was humbled by the generosity and teamwork of these total strangers. And struck by guilt at the way Cole was stepping up, when only a few minutes before she'd been so convinced he was going to abandon her that she'd been willing to risk everything to stop him.

The weight of the straw bag on her shoulder reminded her of the item she'd slipped inside it earlier to ensure his cooperation, but she pushed regret aside to leave her information for the sheriff. As soon as she was done, she and Cole rushed back to the truck, though this time she insisted on climbing inside on her own power.

Heading in the direction Clem had indicated, they quickly turned onto an even smaller, southbound county road that Lisa had never before noticed, much less traveled. Out here, there were no streetlights, and the few houses were flanked by barns and other outbuildings. Stars were popping in the cloudless night sky, more of them by the minute, but they did little to relieve the gathering darkness, or the even bleaker blackness threatening to swamp her.

She couldn't stand to think of how Tyler must be feeling tonight, scared and alone with those two monsters who'd taken him. Couldn't put it out of her mind, not even when Rowdy jumped onto the seat and nuzzled her hand, offering whatever small solace he could.

"They could have split up," she said, her voice shaking. "What if that woman took Tyler with her and went the other way in my car?"

"I expect they've ditched your car somewhere nearby," Cole told her. "Probably figured it's too hot to keep driving. We can catch them, Lisa. If Clem's right about how long ago his Explorer was taken, they're only fifteen or twenty minutes ahead of us, maybe less, since they had your car to deal with."

They drove on, the bumping of the tires on the rutted pavement like an endlessly repeating song.

When she could endure it no longer, she asked, "Would you like a soda?"

"Yeah, sure—or better yet, one of those sports drinks. And you should try to eat and drink, too."

"Forget that," she said as she passed him a chilled bottle. "I'll have something as soon as we find Tyler."

"You need to fuel up now so you won't keel over."

The idea turned her stomach, but she took out a couple of wrapped ham sandwiches, passing one to Cole. Rowdy licked her hand, then softly snuffled, reminding her that he was hungry, too.

She groaned, her stomach pitching.

"Are you okay?" Cole asked.

"Tyler asked me for fast food." Her vision hazed with moist heat. "I told him no, that I'd make dinner. I should have bought him something, should never have told him no."

"I don't know much about you, Lisa," Cole said softly. "But everything I've seen tells me one thing. You're a good mom."

The kindness in his voice was nearly her undoing. She didn't want his compassion, didn't need his understanding. She wanted to hate him, to have someone to blame as much as she blamed herself.

"Before my husband left for his deployment, I told him not to worry about Tyler. I said I would take care of our son so Devin could focus on taking care of himself. I *promised.*"

Cole speared her with a look. "What happened today," he said, his gray eyes troubled, "is wrong. It's as evil as anything I've seen in wartime. But get this in your head, Lisa. It isn't because of anything you did or didn't do."

As his words sank in, they triggered a memory that pushed beyond the aching in her temples. The memory of asking Evie if the abduction was because of something she herself had done.

"The thing is… Remember how you asked if I knew them? Well, I think I do know *her*," Lisa blurted. "The woman who kidnapped us."

"Are you sure?" Cole asked. "Where do you know her from?"

She shook her head. "I can't—I can't remember. She called herself Evie LeStrange, but it was obviously a fake name. When I thought I recognized her, I tried to ask, to find out if I'd somehow done something to offend her. That's when she hit me with her gun."

"Tell me what she looked like, in as much detail as you can remember. Maybe that'll help to jog your memory."

Nodding, Lisa described the hacked, blue-streaked hair and the cruelly thin face, the blue eyes, the black clothing and the sneer. The more she recalled, the more convinced she became that something familiar lay behind the dark facade. "I'm sure of it now," she erupted in frustration. "If only I could remember."

"Could the name have some significance? Maybe it's a reference to something. Have you ever known anyone named Eve, Eva, Evita...?"

Lisa shook her head. "I don't think so."

"What about LeStrange? Could it mean anything?"

She tried to focus, but nothing came to her. When Rowdy whined, she absently pulled out a second sandwich and clumsily unwrapped it, then fed him small pieces. "There's something about her, but the harder I try to think," she said, "the further it slips away."

"Then quit trying," Cole suggested, "and maybe it'll pop into your head a little later."

As they drove on, Lisa wondered how much longer he would be willing to keep driving, how much more he would risk for a fight that wasn't his. And how long it would take him to notice that earlier she'd pulled his gun from beneath the seat and slipped it into her bag in case he changed his mind.

THEY'D GOTTEN DAMNED LUCKY at the last stop, Cole realized, just as they'd been fortunate when Lisa had spotted the dog.

But luck was like that sometimes, lulling the man who counted on it into the false sense that the breaks would always fall his way.

Cole wasn't such a man, and he knew better than to believe, as Lisa seemed to, that all their problems would be over once they caught up with the Explorer. On the contrary, he feared that would be by far the most dangerous part of the equation.

He slid a look to Lisa, who was trying to force down

a bite of sandwich while the little dog wagged his tail and stared plaintively, his front paws on her knee. He should have left both of them back there, where the kind people from the store could have gotten her help. Where she would be out of harm's way while he did whatever he had to.

But her stake in this was so high, he hadn't had it in him to deny her need to be here. That didn't mean, however, that he would brook any interference with the rescue of her son.

"When we catch up with them," he told her, "we're not going to engage. Not until the authorities catch up."

She put down the sandwich and glared at him. "You have to be kidding. We haven't gotten this far just to *follow* them. Heaven only knows what they're doing to my—"

"Do you want him back alive?" He spoke sharply, meaning to shock her. Judging from the devastation in her eyes, it had worked. "If we try to chase them, they might kill him. Or *we* might, if we make whoever's driving wreck the vehicle."

She chewed her lower lip, her eyes brimming. "Then what do we do?"

"Try to maintain visual contact without arousing their suspicions, and let the authorities know where they can find us."

Pulling the phone from her bag, she looked down at it. "No bars at all. No signal."

"Keep checking. We'll get one eventually, or, if we're lucky, the sheriff's deputies will find us first."

"And if they don't?"

"We wait for an opportunity. A chance for me to take out one or both kidnappers." He leaned forward, hunching over the wheel and staring at a flickering glow on the horizon, dark smoke billowing above it. "Look. Look up ahead. What the hell *is* that?"

Images roared up from his past: a crowded market-place, the terrified, dark eyes of a woman in her clean white burka, a split second's hesitation, then the distant concussion as the scene—along with Lisa's husband and a dozen innocent civilian shoppers—erupted into flame.

But this was not Afghanistan, he knew, so he shunted the painful memory aside and rounded the curve, already feeling the horror tightening in his gut. Already smelling the smoke as the rear end of a burning vehicle, its nose down in a roadside ditch, came into view.

"That's my car!" screamed Lisa, though only the blazing trunk was visible. "Oh, my God, Tyler could be in there! He might be locked inside!"

Chapter Six

"Stay in the truck," Cole ordered as he parked the vehicle as close to the fire as he dared. "Don't you move from this spot, and I mean it."

Maybe it was his tone, and maybe it was shock, but Lisa froze where she sat, her gaze locked on the hungry flames consuming the car.

It was altogether possible the fuel tank would blow at any minute. And altogether probable that no living child was inside. But he had come this far already, had become—no matter how he'd tried to steel himself against it—emotionally invested. There was no way he could live with himself if he simply sat and watched the car burn.

He didn't have an extinguisher, but the toolbox he'd been using earlier to fix up old bikes for the children of deployed soldiers was still in the back of the truck. He found a hammer to break out a window and then took off at a run, his body bent as low as he could manage.

As he approached the blaze, the heat was so intense, he instinctively shielded his face with his jacket-clad arm to protect it. Jumping across the ditch some thirty feet distant, he approached the sedan's nose-down front end which appeared to be less heavily involved. He choked on the acrid black smoke and pressed forward, his eyes, nose streaming from the fumes. By the time, close enough to see that the front door had been left wide open, he felt intense heat on his exposed hand and smelled the distinctive stench of burned hair. It had to be his own.

Knowing he could ignite at any moment, he forced himself another few steps forward, his breath held to spare his lungs from the hot gases that would sear them. It was almost impossible to see, with smoke and fire pouring from inside the vehicle, and he could barely force his eyes open wide enough to make out anything at all.

Finally there was an instant where the flames twisted and the smoke billowed and he clearly saw that the required car seat wasn't in the vehicle. The kidnappers must have moved it, along with the child, into the SUV they'd stolen.

Dark as it was, he made out one other detail: the firelight reflecting off a candy wrapper lying in the grass beside the car. Then the heat and smoke forced him back to where he coughed and choked, resting his hands on his knees for support. He thought of making a second run at the car, but it was hopeless, and getting himself killed would serve nobody's interests.

"Cole, your jacket—you're on fire!" Lisa warned, coming up behind him and beating out the flames on his sleeve with the army blanket she'd brought from the truck.

When he could manage it, he peeled off his jacket, then dropped it on the ground and stamped the smoldering fabric with his boot.

Ignoring it, he told Lisa, "There's nobody inside. No car seat, either. You did have one for him, right?"

"What about the trunk?" she asked.

"It must have popped open in the crash. I didn't see ᵍg inside."

dded, eyes closing. "Thank God, and thank

you, Cole. I won't forget you risked your life. Are you all right?"

"Come on," he said, his voice hoarse from the smoke. "Back to the truck. Burning cars don't blow up often, but it's not a chance we need to take."

He picked up the jacket and took it with him. Partially burned sleeve or not, he didn't rule out the possibility that he might need it later.

Inside the truck, he backed a safe distance down the road, then put the transmission back into Park and dragged in several deep breaths between fits of coughing.

"Here." Reaching past the quivering dog, Lisa handed him some water and the first-aid kit he'd left on the floorboard earlier. "Maybe there's some ointment. Your hand and arm are red, and those are blisters coming up."

He spared the burns a glance and did a quick assessment. They hurt like hell, but in this case, that was a good thing, meaning that the nerves remained intact. "It's only first-degree," he said, though he knew the blisters indicated second. "I'll deal with it later."

"So, why are we stopping? You said yourself, they can't be far ahead."

He shook his head. "Deputies'll be here soon. Dark as it is out here, the light from that fire will be visible for miles."

She shook her head. "No, we can't wait for them. Every second we delay puts us farther behind."

"You need to listen to me, Lisa. The sheriff's department knows this county, and they have the resources to head off those people, maybe even call out a chopper from the state or bring the feds in on this. And if it comes down to a hostage negotiation, they're far better equipped than two injured civilians."

"You're not a civilian," she challenged. "You're a Ranger."

"An *ex*-Ranger," he corrected, the admission twisting like a knife in his chest. "A failed Ranger."

"Really? Well, the way you played the hero at the bank, I don't buy the *failed* part for a second. You could do this if you wanted to. You could save my son."

He winced at the reminder of everything that his misguided heroics had cost them. A fresh start with the U.S. Marshals in his case. A five-year-old son in hers. The botched bank robbery had been the Afghan market in Lashkar Gah all over again, only this time it hadn't been his hesitation but his rash act that had cost Lisa Meador a member of her family.

You should tell her who she's dealing with. Tell her everything.

But his C.O.'s words came back to haunt him, and he told himself she had more than enough to contend with already. Unable to meet her eyes, he looked away, in the direction of the fire. In the time it took to mark her swift movement in his peripheral vision, she managed to pull a gun from her straw bag.

His Glock. When in hell had she had the time to pull it out from under his seat? And even as desperate as she was to get to her son, did she really have it in her to shoot him and drive off in his truck?

"IF YOU DON'T want to help me, you can wait here alone for the deputies," Lisa told him, her voice as hard as she could manage to make up for the shaking of her left hand. "Now, either drive or get out, and I'll take it from here."

The look that flashed across his features was incredulous. "You're kidding, right? One minute you're beating out a fire to keep me from burning and telling me you won't forget what I did, and now you're pulling my own gun on me?"

"With or without your help, I'm going to find Tyler," she said, ignoring the dog's nervous whining. She understood the animal's fear—her heart was jumping around in her chest like a terrified jackrabbit—but she couldn't allow anyone or anything to stop her.

"You'll get yourself killed. And maybe Tyler, too." Cole studied her intently, his gray eyes reflecting the fire ahead. "Are you willing to live with that risk, Lisa? And the consequences? Because I can tell you, that kind of regret's the real hell. One that's a million times worse than getting yourself shot down."

She hesitated at his questions, at the sense of loss, the torment, that radiated from his voice. But finally she nodded. "When my husband died, there was nothing I could do about it. No way to go back in time to warn him about the suicide bomber, or even to give him one last kiss before he went out to patrol that marketplace. It's been thirteen months, and I still have the same nightmares, where I'm flossing a patient's teeth or buying groceries, clueless, while on another screen in my head, he's dying with those other people. I can't—I *won't*—live with thinking I might have those same dreams about our son. With knowing I might not be there when he needs me most."

He looked directly into her eyes, and she would have sworn that she felt some kind of connection, the shared understanding that both of them had suffered a loss so catastrophic it forever shattered the world as they had known it. For a moment she thought that shared bond might make a difference, until he looked away.

So that was it. He wasn't going to help her. Disappointment overwhelmed her. And then he spoke again.

"All right, Lisa," he said quietly, then cleared his throat.

"We're going. But only if you put away that damned gun before you hurt somebody."

She leaned over to drop it in her bag—which he snatched away from her so quickly that Rowdy yipped in alarm.

He shoved the gun into the well on the door, well out of her reach, then handed back the bag and cut her a look that brimmed with masculine irritation. A look that assured her that her rash act had cut off their still-fragile connection at the knees.

"Pull that sort of stunt on me again—" he spat out the words, scowling "—and I'm shoving your ass out of the truck and leaving you to fend for yourself. You understand me?"

Terrified as she was, she couldn't swallow, much less respond in any way. Couldn't even breathe until he put the truck back into gear and drove off in the direction the kidnappers must have taken.

So FAR, SO GOOD, thought Deputy Trace Sutherland as he and his wife—no, his *ex*-wife—sped toward the interstate. After coming to a fork in the road, he and Jill had managed a stiff but still-professional discussion before agreeing that Cole Sawyer would have wanted to bypass the frequent speed zones along the smaller roads. Whether he was heading due west or meant to turn south to cross the border into Mexico, as Trace thought likely, he was clearly in one hell of a hurry.

They had long since left Tuller County and the reach of their radio far behind, so Jill called in to Dispatch the moment she realized that she had cell phone reception. After a brief conversation, she covered the receiver and said, "They're patching me through to the sheriff."

"Put the phone on Speaker, will you?"

Her expression soured in an instant. "Give me a little credit, will you, Sutherland? I was just about to do that."

Her use of his last name—a name that they'd once shared—stung worse than the criticism.

"Thanks, Jill," he murmured.

Once he would have risen to the bait, would have sarcastically tossed back her newly reclaimed maiden name to inflict his fair share of damage. But in the eight months since that dark day their divorce became final, he'd lost his taste for that particular blood sport. Mostly because he'd been the one left bleeding.

He wondered if Jill still cared, even a little, or if she had eased her suffering with another man yet. Painful as the thought was, he was well aware that her tall blond good looks and outsize personality had always attracted admiration. But if she had a boyfriend, no one had dared mention it to him, and he rarely saw her since he'd transferred to another shift. He'd moved across town, too, from the house they had once shared. The house that had been a home until the day a drunken fool named Jimmy James Barlow almost killed her.

Sheriff Hank Stewart came on the line. As usual, he got straight down to business. "What's your twenty, Keller?"

"We're nearly at the ramp onto Interstate 10," Jill said.

"You need to turn around right now and get over to the Texas Two-Step in Coffee Creek." He gave them directions, naming the state road they had passed up.

"Got it." She scowled, and Trace grimaced, remembering the sign they'd bypassed.

With no other cars in sight, he made a quick three-point turn on the narrow road.

"Just got a call from the Farris County sheriff," Stewart went on. "Our suspect and the injured female came in with some wild story about a carjacking. Claimed the kidnappers took off with the woman's five-year-old kid."

"So the silver Camry they were chasing is hers?" Trace's gut tightened at the news. True or not, the possibility of a child abduction took this pursuit to a whole new level. What he couldn't figure out was how that story fit in with the botched bank robbery.

"A local deputy just radioed in to Dispatch," their boss told them. "According to the sheriff, his deputy found the vehicle burning over on County Road…something or other. I've got it written down here somewhere." They heard papers shuffling, and then he gave the number, which Jill quickly jotted on the pad she'd pulled from her breast pocket.

"So you think our suspect caught up with these alleged kidnappers and dealt some homegrown justice?" Trace asked.

"Can't say for sure, since the deputy can't get close enough to check for bodies, but I doubt it," the sheriff answered. "Some fella at the Two-Step got his vehicle stolen just before our suspect, who it turns out really is an ex-Ranger by the name of Cole Sawyer, and the injured woman came into the store. The woman claimed the car thief's description matched that of her carjacker."

"Do you have the stolen vehicle's description?" Jill asked.

"Four-year-old dark blue Ford Explorer." He rattled off the plate number but had to repeat it when static broke up his words, since they were traveling farther away from the closest cell tower. "The woman at…Two-Step may have…information for you. Go…interview…before…decide how to proceed."

Trace opened his mouth to acknowledge the order before they lost the signal, but, as usual, Jill was quicker on the draw.

"Wouldn't we be better off letting Farris County handle that and continuing our pursuit of the bank robber? After all, we have to be a heck of a lot closer than they are, and if there's really a kid somewhere in all this, time is of the essence."

Trace winced, almost certain that the sheriff—always quick to anger when he thought his orders were being questioned—was about to blast her. But the only thing that came through before they lost the connection was a garbled version of *"Proceed as..."*

"You think he meant *proceed as ordered?*" Trace asked, thinking, from the tone of their boss's voice, that they'd probably missed out on a few expletives.

"Oh, noooo." When Jill grinned in his direction, for just a moment, he felt as if he had his gung-ho, risk-anything-for-results wife back, as if Jimmy James Barlow, the arguments and the divorce had never happened. And he would swear, she'd never been more beautiful, more alive, than she looked now. "I'm positive that he meant we should proceed with my idea. We can catch them, Trace. We can bring them in."

If he had any sense at all, he would have backtracked until they got a signal, or out-and-out ignored her ridiculous suggestion. But because she'd used his first name this time, though he had never been one for pissing off the sheriff who'd taught him so much, he decided he was going along for the ride.

He had to, with his instincts screaming like a thousand sirens that in this case, on this night, there were far more important things than his career at stake.

Chapter Seven

Still floating from a fresh high, Lee Ray pictured the car as it had gone up, the barbecue starter fluid making a loud *whoosh* as it ignited, the flames billowing and the black smoke rolling as thick as his relief. He'd been scared as hell, his guts churning, when Evie pulled the plastic bottle from her "bag of tricks," as he thought of her duffel.

Just as she'd demanded, he had gotten the Explorer, then met her on this godforsaken stretch of road. But his obedience didn't guarantee she wouldn't suddenly douse him and light him up with a casually flicked cigarette—and it sure as hell wouldn't protect the boy still sleeping in the backseat.

With his long lashes and his small arm wrapped around his stuffed toy, the child stirred a memory Lee Ray had thought he'd put behind him, of the kid he'd left behind back in Corpus Christi. A snot-nosed little rug rat Lee Ray had told himself would be better off without a crankhead convict for a father.

After leaving the brat's mother with nothing but an empty wallet, he had given up the right to call and ask her how his kid was doing. And he sure as hell wasn't about to risk his own life to ask Evie to spare the son of a woman she had marked for some bat-shit-crazy brand of payback.

Still, he'd somehow found the balls to remind her that prison was a special brand of hell for baby killers.

Evie had laughed in his face. "Only if you're caught, sweets. But we can worry about that later. For now you can put the kid in our new ride—and don't forget the car seat. We don't want to get pulled over for some dumb-ass little thing like that."

After a time, the miles and the dark road lulled him, and Lee Ray dozed, dreaming of a woman who thought nothing of lighting up the night sky for miles around but worried about being popped over a kiddie car seat, a woman who doled out meth and sex and violent death at her whim.

A series of rough jolts woke him later. It was pitchblack and his high was already fading, leaving him edgy and twitchy and wondering when he could ask for the next tweak. They were pulling off the shoulder, over ruts and behind a screen of scrubby brush.

Killing the headlights, she said, "Wake up and get your gun out, Lee Ray. You're about to need it."

His stomach dropped, and he snapped fully awake— and way too close to stone-cold sober. Did she mean to make him shoot the boy? Had she decided it was time already?

"I—I can't do it," he stammered, cold sweat pouring from his body. "I won't."

She snorted. "If you know what's good for you, you'll do exactly what I tell you. Now grab that gun and get out of the car. At the top of that hill back there, I spotted headlights behind us. Whoever's comin' is closing in too fast to be anything but on our tail—and we can't afford anybody getting between us and our meeting with *El Diablo*."

Lee Ray had no idea who this *El Diablo* was. Some Mexican drug lord, maybe, that no sane person would get within a hundred miles of, but for all he knew, it could be some story Evie'd dreamed up, a figment of her imagination that was subject to change at any moment. He wasn't sure, either, that she was right about them being followed, but he knew better than to argue with her paranoia, especially when he saw her pull another weapon from the duffel on the seat beside her.

He blinked and squinted, then finally recognized the silhouette of what could only be an assault rifle, a gun that he had never seen before. A gun that made his .38 look as effective as a flyswatter in comparison.

"Come on, and let's get set. Your little pet back there'll be just fine. Probably won't even wake up when we start shooting."

His bowels turned to ice water. "We're—we're shooting at the *cops?*"

"We're shooting at anybody I say, and I'm telling you, whoever's coming up behind us has to die."

He glanced down at his weapon. Why hadn't he used it on her while he could? He could've taken all the crank and left the kid someplace where he'd be found safe. All it would have taken was a single bullet—

But Lee Ray didn't have the guts to complete the thought, much less defy the woman he could not imagine ever leaving. Instead, he followed her directions, the last of his high ruined by the knowledge that, despite his pathetic protests, there was absolutely nothing, no matter how depraved or violent, she could not force him to do.

THOUGH THE TERRAIN HAD gotten hillier, every so often Cole caught a fleeting flash of distant taillights. Most likely the kidnappers, but he could not be absolutely certain. He might have fallen in behind a driver who'd turned onto this road at one of the small intersections they had passed, just as it was possible that his targets had turned off and he'd lost them.

Still, at this time of night, he didn't think so, and his gut told him that after hours of hard driving, they were finally getting close. He just had to be certain.

"Any signal on that phone yet?" he asked Lisa, whose head had drooped.

"Wha—" She jerked awake in an instant, then groaned, her hand shooting to her upper arm. "Ow. How long have I been sleeping? Have we caught up yet?"

"Not so long, and maybe. Why don't you take a couple more pain pills, maybe take the edge off?"

Ignoring the suggestion, she leaned forward. "Where are they?"

"I can't guarantee it's them, but I've seen taillights up ahead. Whoever's up there is traveling at a pretty good clip, too." He prayed that he was right, that they hadn't been chasing some random back-road traveler in a hurry, maybe some coyote smuggling illegals or a drug runner, either of which could be every bit as dangerous as the people they were after.

"It has to be them. I just know it."

"Check the phone," he reminded her. "This would be a really good time to arrange some backup."

"Right." She pulled it from the straw bag and peered down at its face. "Two, no, there's just one bar. I'm trying 9-1-1." She stared at the phone as if willing it to obey her. "Come on, come on," she murmured. "Connect already, please… Hello? This is Lisa Meador from Coopersville, and my five-year-old son has been kidnapped. We're following the SUV they took, and— Do you know where we are, Cole?"

Cole was from California, and he wasn't familiar with this part of Texas, but he gave the number he'd seen on the road sign, along with the name of a state park they'd passed.

Lisa relayed the information before saying, "It's not my phone. I don't know the number— Hello?"

A long pause was followed by "Are you still there? Please? Oh, *shoot!*"

As if on cue, the moment the word escaped her lips, what could only be automatic gunfire shattered the night's stillness. At the edge of his vision, Cole caught the muzzle flashes at the same moment his right front tire blew out and more rounds punched along the truck's flank— including one that slammed straight through the door and into the dashboard just above the dog's head.

The animal yelped and Lisa screamed, but Cole had no time to wonder whether she'd been hit. He was too busy wrestling the wheel to keep the speeding, swerving truck from overturning.

As fast as he reacted, the truck reacted to the blowout faster, its rear end slewing around, and the tires squealing and bumping off the pavement. He tried to steer into the spin, but it was no use. The pickup bucked and bounced off the road, until the undercarriage crunched hard against something solid and jerked them to a brutal stop.

He killed the lights and ducked, feeling around until he found his pistol. Not that it would do him much good against the kind of weapon capable of the rapid gunfire that had taken them off the road.

"You all right, Lisa?" Heart pounding wildly, he struggled to get a lock on his emotions.

His only answer was her moan and the dog's whining, though Rowdy sounded far more terrified than hurt.

"Were you hit?" He couldn't see her in the darkness, but he reached out and felt her shoulder and realized she was lying across the seat.

At his touch, she lurched upright. "I'm not hit. What about you? Are you all right?"

"Yeah, but we won't be if they come up on us in the dark. Out of the truck right now—and leave the dog. He'll give away our location with his whining."

"But Rowdy's scared to death. I can't just—"

"If he gets the two of us killed, your son's got no one." Cole flipped off the dome light so it wouldn't silhouette them when the doors opened. "No one except that pair of—"

"I'm so sorry, boy," she said. "Stay, Rowdy." After tucking the blanket around the dog, she bailed out of the truck and quietly closed the door behind her.

Cole joined her, worried because he hadn't seen or heard anyone drive off.

Which meant the two criminals were hunting them in the darkness, with firepower far superior to his.

But he seriously doubted the kidnappers Lisa had described had anything close to his experience stalking human prey in rough terrain. Nor would they share his ability to move with silent stealth.

Lisa didn't share it, either, he discovered as she stumbled over loose rocks that clattered noisily as she sucked in an audible breath. Taking her by the elbow, he led her toward a rocky outcrop he had noticed in the headlights moments earlier.

Leaning close to her ear, he whispered, "Guess you must've slept through night maneuvers training class at dental hygiene school."

At her exasperated sigh, a grin tugged at the corner his mouth, and he realized that for the first time since Lashkar Gah, he was feeling the old rush that his career once gave him, an exhilaration he'd feared was lost forever.

After months of feeling dead inside, it was one hell of

a relief. But he could not forget for a single second his obligation to the terrified woman at his side or the child they were both intent on saving.

He stooped to pick up several fist-size stones. One by one, he chunked them toward a spot between where the truck had come to rest and where he thought the shooter had been. Maybe the noise would at least distract them for a minute.

Unless, of course, they had night-vision goggles to go with their military-style weapon. If that was the case, the kidnappers could gun them down before they knew what hit them.

Overhead, he spotted the white flare of a meteor before it faded against a backdrop filled with more stars than any city dweller could imagine. Though the moon had not yet risen, now that his eyes had adjusted he made out the individual silhouettes of rocks and a few clumps of scrubby trees.

"Over here," he said, leading her toward one of the latter. "Now duck under those branches and get over there, behind that rock, and keep still." There, at least, she would have some cover, and he wouldn't have to worry that she might make noise and draw fire.

"We're not just hiding, are we?" The worry in her voice was palpable. "Not with Tyler so close."

"You might not've noticed, but they aren't exactly packing peashooters. So *you* are waiting here and staying put until I come to get you."

She hesitated before saying, "What if you don't come back?"

For just a moment he wondered if at least a little of the worry shading her voice could be on his account. But that was ridiculous. She was only worried about losing her best chance of saving the child whose life meant more to her than her own, not a man she barely knew.

He pulled the keys out of his pocket, his hand gripping them carefully to keep them from jingling. "Here, take these, but promise me you'll wait until first light before you even *think* of going back to the truck." He prayed that the vehicle was still drivable. "Until then, don't move a muscle, no matter what you hear, no matter what they threaten."

"What if they…what if they say they'll kill you?"

So she *was* worried about him—him, of all people. "I swear to you," he promised, "they aren't taking me alive."

"And Tyler? I can't just hide if they start threatening to hurt him."

"If they still have your son—and I have no reason to think otherwise—they don't want him dead. Otherwise they would never have risked the heat a child abduction's sure to bring down." Cole didn't want to think about what they could want with an innocent five-year-old. "But they'll kill you in a second if you show yourself. You understand that?"

When she nodded, he pressed the keys into her left hand.

To his surprise, her fingers threaded through his and she squeezed them, the keys digging into both their palms. "Cole," she whispered, "I'm so sorry. Sorry for dragging you into—"

"Like you said before, I did it to myself the moment I decided to try to stop that robbery. If I'd had any way of knowing… I'm sorry, Lisa—sorrier than you'll ever know." *And sorrier still for what I haven't told you.*

"Don't. Please." She raised herself onto her toes and brushed the fullness of her warm lips across his. The kiss was soft and fleeting—meaningless, really, in the heat

ehow it sent a jolt that
as if he'd never expe-
Desire gripped him, a
her mouth in earnest, to
r that had somehow stirred
s once his beating heart.
to regain his composure, then
he wave of shame that followed.
e world… This was Staff Sergeant
ow, for heaven's sake. How sick was
ing for her but remorse?

r you," Cole managed, his voice rough.
there's any way—any way at all—to make
l be bringing your son with me. Just think of
thing else. Think of Tyler back in your arms."

Before she could answer, or do anything else to throw off his equilibrium, he turned and melted into the shadows, becoming one with the cool darkness of the Texas night.

"Don't answer it," Jill pleaded as Trace reached for the radio handset.

But with the local emergency services dispatcher telling them he was patching through a call from Sheriff Stewart himself on a designated channel, it wasn't as if he had a choice.

"If we don't respond," she went on, reaching for the off switch, "he'll just think we're out of radio range."

When he grabbed her hand to stop her, the shock of their contact, after so many long months of avoiding even the sight of each other, jolted through him like an electric charge. "If you think that, you don't know Hank Stewart," he told her, remembering how much her tendency to play the rogue cop had already cost them. "And if you

think I'm irresponsible enough to break m
you don't know your ex-husband, either."

She let her hand fall to her lap and speared
look so openly hostile, he realized he'd been f
self with his insane hopes for a reunion. She
going to forgive him for the ultimatum he had l
and he was never going to see his way past th
give it in the first place.

Hank Stewart's voice came on the radio, sp
far too clearly to be misunderstood. "Deputies S
land and Keller, I have some additional informatio
you on our suspect and the woman traveling with hi
including the number to a cell phone given to her by
owner of the Texas Two-Step back in Coffee Creek. I ha
new orders for you, too, and this time, you'd damned wel
better listen if you mean to keep your jobs."

Chapter Eight

Cole grinned, realizing that at least one of the kidnappers was even noisier than Lisa, who was stashed safely not sixty yards from the spot where the target was moving. If the criminals were together, this was going to be one easy takedown.

If he'd been on the battlefield, he might have opted to cover a mouth and slit a throat, allowing him to quickly and silently dispatch the first kidnapper and move on to the next. But in this situation he might need intel on the location of the second criminal or even Tyler, if he'd been wrong about the boy being somewhere nearby, still in the stolen Explorer.

Besides, he was no longer sanctioned by the government to kill as he judged necessary in the service of his mission. As a civilian, he knew his every action would be scrutinized, and the loss of his chance to become a U.S. Marshal was nothing compared to the unthinkable threat of losing his own freedom if his conduct was deemed criminal.

But criminal or not, the debt he owed to the family of Staff Sergeant Devin Meador burned like a live coal in his belly, and he knew that whatever it ended up costing him, he was prepared to pay the price.

Staying low and upwind of his quarry, he closed in

from behind. Both training and instinct had him seeking out any shrub or rock that might camouflage his own clearly human silhouette, but he needn't have bothered. His stumbling, shambling target never turned his head to look.

As he moved to within twenty yards, Cole could easily make out the smoky stench of unwashed flesh—probably the male, judging from the shape and height. It took only another moment to determine that his opponent was substantially shorter and skinnier than he was, and clearly in no condition to prevail in a hand-to-hand confrontation.

Though Cole couldn't make out whether the man was armed, he appeared to be alone. The question was, was his female partner in the SUV with Tyler, or was she close enough to open fire if she heard a commotion?

With no way to be certain, Cole moved within striking range, his muscles poised for release like hundreds of drawn bowstrings. He focused, mind and body, then drew a steadying breath.

And stiffened, horror jolting through him at the sound of a ringing phone.

TWENTY MINUTES OF crouching behind the rock, hunched beneath the sharp thorns of the twisted limbs of a low-growing mesquite tree, had left Lisa stiff in every muscle. Still in pain from both the bullet wound to her arm and the blow to her head, she was freezing, too, as the temperature dropped. She wished in vain for the blanket she'd foolishly left with Rowdy in the truck. But mostly she was terrified of what might be happening while she sat there shivering like a coward, so close to her son and so maddeningly dependent on another person to get near him....

Even if that person was a man as brave and capable as Captain Cole Sawyer.

At least, she prayed he was capable as all her instincts screamed that he was. But Devin, too, had seemed so strong, so confident in both his training and his fellow soldiers, when he'd assured her he would return to her and Tyler alive. She'd believed in him wholeheartedly, had trusted in his strength and her faith to shield him from all harm.

Her cold fingers drifted to her lips, the same lips that had kissed her husband goodbye on their last day together. She had kissed Cole Sawyer, too. What on earth had she been thinking?

Nothing. Nothing at all. Certainly she hadn't been confusing a man she'd known for only hours with the husband whose death was still a raw wound.

That simple kiss had only been meant to wish Cole good luck, to thank him for risking his life to save the son who was her whole world. Anything else was unthinkable. It had been nothing more than a fleeting peck that meant less than when she'd kissed her father goodbye the last time he'd come for a visit.

It was only this horrible situation, not the man involved, that had dredged up this riot of emotion—and what she felt was nothing compared to the terror that weakened her knees each time she thought of what might be happening to Tyler.

For the third time since Cole had left she checked the borrowed cell phone for a signal. If she held it at exactly the right angle, the tiny screen showed one bar, so she tried to call the emergency operator again. But she couldn't get the call to go through, no matter how she shifted her position.

Maybe if she made her way onto the rocky outcrop she'd seen, she could get an unobstructed signal. But climbing up would mean leaving the spot where she had promised Cole she would wait, the place where he had vowed to do his best to bring Tyler. It was the risk of somehow missing him, more than the idea of making noise that would attract the attention of the shooter, that kept her anchored in place.

Finally, though, she just had to stretch her cramped muscles, and as carefully as she could, she stretched her right leg, then stiffened as her foot bumped against something in the leaf litter near the rock's base.

It was a cool night, far too cool for snakes to be active. But she must have disturbed a sleeping rattler, and at the sound of its distinctive warning, raw instinct took over, and she started racing for the outcrop.

She didn't even realize she'd dropped the cell phone until it started ringing and the night erupted into gunfire.

COLE SILENTLY cursed himself for neglecting to warn Lisa to put the phone into silent mode, but he barely had time to finish the thought as a harsh burst of automatic gunfire split the night from somewhere off to his left.

Lisa! His every protective instinct urged him to go to her, even though training and common sense insisted that he first had to deal with the one threat within reach.

He did what he had to, striking his target like a guided missile and slamming the man's head onto the ground with such speed and force that he was unconscious before he knew what hit him. Relieving the criminal of his handgun, Cole strained his ears for any sign of Evie. She might have stopped shooting to reload, or she could merely be waiting, listening as he was for any sign of movement.

Except in her case, she would be straining to hear signs of life from the woman she had surely shot down. The woman he should have safeguarded but had instead left behind him, a sitting target.

As he slipped through the darkness toward Lisa's position, Cole was powerless to stop the waves of guilt rippling through him and the dread whispering that no matter how brave and determined Lisa was, she was no soldier. When that phone started ringing and the shooting began, instinct would have had her running like a rabbit— a rabbit to be slaughtered in a hail of gunfire.

A nightmare image flashed through his brain, a vision of her crumpled body, blood flowing like dark streamers from half a dozen wounds. In that moment, he wanted nothing so much as to get his hands on Evie LeStrange, to rip the gun from her hands and beat her with it until he caved in her sadistic skull. As deeply ingrained in him as it was to never harm a female, this cruel creature was no woman, was barely even the same species as the beautiful and loving mother she had callously fired on.

Cole had been on missions when friends he'd lived with, fought with, bled with for years had made the final sacrifice. In the heat of battle, all emotion had to go on lockdown, had to give way to a mission that mattered more than any individual, or even the entire team.

But this time, he couldn't do it, couldn't make himself forget Lisa's sweet kiss or the longing she'd awakened. As wrong as it had been to want her, the pain of her loss poured through him like an icy river, so stark and cold and real that he wanted to curse her for making him feel anything at all.

Wrenching himself back into the here and now, he reminded himself that right now Lisa's son *was* the mission. If Tyler disappeared or died, her sacrifice would be for nothing.

Focusing on a goal helped Cole shake off his paralysis, and he forced himself to move on. His teeth gritted, he circled around to flank the woman with the AK-47, a gun in each of his hands and murder on his mind.

THROWING HERSELF to the ground as the first shots rang out, Lisa lay still, her heart pounding like a war drum as her nails dug into the hillside's gritty soil. She felt as much as heard the deep *thunk* of bullets drilling the ground behind her, and her eyes clenched shut, her entire body tensing against the expectation that she would die at any second.

The impact never came, and the night once more fell silent. Except for the uncontrollable shaking that gripped her, Lisa couldn't move, could barely breathe, could think of nothing but the way one misstep and an angry rattler had combined to save her life.

But only if she didn't call attention to herself now.

As the seconds crawled past, she began to wonder if the shooter was coming this way to check for a body. Would they stop searching once they found the phone, or keep on going until they found her?

Desperately, she wished she had Cole by her side, if only so she could ask him what her next move should be. Even the thought of him somewhere nearby reassured her just a little. Refusing to consider the possibility that he might have been killed or injured, she instead imagined him, calm and strong and confident, as he drew a bead on the shooter. She pictured the scene in such vivid detail that she braced herself for the quick pop of his handgun.

Instead, she heard nothing but the stirring of a cool breeze and the rusted-hinge screeching of a distant owl. But she saw something when she dared to open her eyes again. A crescent moon had risen in the eastern sky.

Higher in elevation, since she'd made it halfway to the rocky outcrop, she made out something gleaming in the thin light. Something metallic, she was almost certain.

Something like… Holding her breath, she dared to lift her head to look and saw that, yes, it was a bumper. The bumper of a vehicle parked perhaps a hundred yards from where Cole's truck had ended up.

It had to be the stolen Explorer. And every cell and synapse in her screamed that Tyler was inside it, clutching his stuffed octopus as he waited for her to come find him.

Like a wind dispersing smoke, the thought cleared away all indecision. She had to get down to that vehicle. Had to save her son.

And somehow she had to do it without getting either of them killed.

Chapter Nine

"He jumped me, Evie! Wasn't my fault! And the bastard's got my gun!"

Cole swore when he heard the shouting and realized he hadn't hit the tattooed kidnapper nearly hard enough. The terror in the man's words also confirmed that the AK-47-toting "Evie" completely dominated her male partner—a role reversal that shattered Cole's hopes that she might possess enough maternal instincts to protect a helpless child.

Ignoring the now-unarmed man blundering through the darkness, Cole continued moving toward a point between where Evie had been shooting and the spot where he'd left Lisa. The place where his target might be heading to confirm her kill.

If he had anything to say about it, Evie would die there, because he was far too angry to give a damn about staying out of trouble any longer.

A sound drew his attention, the subtle clatter of one pebble kicked against another. Zeroing in on it, he was soon rewarded with a glimpse of a curvy form he recognized as female.

Taking aim, he hesitated, wondering if Tattoo Man could possibly find his way back to the SUV and escape with Tyler if startled by the sound of gunfire. Quickly, he dismissed that concern, figuring he could head off the injured man before he got that far.

An instant before he squeezed the trigger, he caught the soft scent of vanilla on the breeze. *Lisa's* scent, he realized, his heart flooding with relief that she was still alive and gratitude that he hadn't shot her for a second time that day.

"Lisa," he whispered as he moved toward her.

She gasped quietly before recovering and clutching his arm tightly. After giving it a squeeze, she let go and pointed off toward his right. "This way," she murmured. "I saw where they're parked."

He nodded, knowing he couldn't possibly leave her again. Even if he found a relatively safe place for her, now that she had spotted the Explorer, nothing he could say would prevent her from heading for her son the moment he was out of sight.

Better they should stay together, taking the chance on getting out of here with Tyler, than continue this deadly game of blind man's bluff with a much better armed opponent.

An opponent who might well possess the cunning to stake out the Explorer and gun them down as they approached.

ALL LISA COULD THINK of was getting Tyler away from danger, holding her son in her arms and never letting go again. But every time it felt as if they were making headway, Cole clamped a firm hand on her forearm, forcing her to stop. She tried in vain to jerk free, wanting to scream that they had to hurry. They needed to run as fast as they could, not creep in the zigzagging course he insisted on, pausing every few feet to listen for any sign of pursuit.

But she didn't say a word. She couldn't, with the sound

of the gunfire still ringing in her ears. Not to mention that if she argued with him, the sound would carry, drawing bullets as surely as the ringing phone had done.

After what felt like the longest, slowest walk of her life, she leaned toward him and whispered, "There," then pointed out a distant, squared-off shape half-hidden by the tall weeds and the shrubs that screened it. Her heart seized when the rear door opened and a tiny silhouette emerged.

"M-mommy? Mommy, where are you?" As slurred and sleepy as the voice was, she knew Tyler when she heard him. Of all the times for him to wriggle out of his seat…

She struggled against Cole's grip, her cry stopped by his hand across her mouth.

"Wait here while I get him," he breathed into her ear. "This could be a trap."

"No!" Even muffled, her cry drew unwanted attention, and she saw someone reach out, grab Tyler and drag him back inside the vehicle.

Releasing her, Cole took off running, making a bee-line for the SUV as it roared to life. As Lisa watched in horror, he took aim at the windshield just as the Explorer swerved hard to the right.

He stood his ground but held his fire as the SUV kept coming, gathering speed as it raced toward him. He must be worried about hitting Tyler, she realized, because he waited, lining up his shot as the high beams nearly blinded both of them.

He finally pulled the trigger, then leaped to one side.

Lisa gasped as a thud told her that he hadn't been quick enough. As he was knocked aside into the darkness, she raced toward him, intent on grabbing his gun and shooting the tires before the kidnappers could get away.

But they were gone before she reached him, bouncing toward the paved road and leaving behind a plume of dust.

She screamed "No!" as Tyler was stolen from her for a second time that day.

Cole's groan dragged her attention from the disappearing taillights. Kneeling down beside him, she wiped away her blinding tears. "Are you all right?"

"Barely clipped my hip. I'll be okay." He struggled to his feet. "Which way did—"

"Back toward the road. Please—we have to catch up."

He limped as they made their way back to his pickup. "Sorry, but we're not going anywhere until I get that tire changed," he said.

The air rushed from her lungs. But he was right. They would never catch up on a blown-out tire. Fighting back tears, she nodded. "Let me help."

She heard another vehicle out on the road, but she couldn't see it. Apparently the driver didn't spot them, either, because the car rushed past without slowing.

Frowning at the receding sound, Cole hurried to get his spare and tools. Despite his injury, he insisted on doing the heavy lifting as they rushed through the task.

Once they finished, Lisa climbed in unassisted, forcing herself to use her injured arm. Rowdy leaped into her lap and snuggled against her, his blond tail wagging.

With a grunt of pain, Cole hoisted himself into his seat and fired up the engine.

"Sure you're okay to drive?" she asked.

"I've got it," he said. But when he put the truck in gear, though the engine revved, they didn't budge.

"What's wrong? Why aren't we moving?" Every second they delayed was ripping her to pieces.

"Either the transmission's gone out," he said as he shifted into Reverse, "or—damn it. I think we're hung up on something."

She felt her hope shatter into a million pieces. "No! This can't be happening."

"Let me just try—" he shifted into Reverse "—backing up. There."

With a thump that shook the whole frame, the truck rolled off whatever had been holding it. Lisa had barely clicked her seat belt before they were bumping over the same rough ground they'd covered when they left the highway.

Once they reached the pavement, he mashed down on the gas. But all too soon, the truck began to shudder, and Cole furiously popped the steering wheel with the back of his hand as they lost speed.

"Damn it," he said. "We must've done some serious damage when we ran off the road. I can't even get it past forty. We'll never catch them like this."

Pain tore through Lisa's center, agony so intense, she wanted to scream with it. There had to be some way to fix this, some way to get help—if only she hadn't dropped the phone.

Of course, if she hadn't, she would be dead. But if she lost her child, what would she have to live for anyway?

She clamped down on the destructive thinking. *I won't give up on you, Tyler. I promise you, I'll find help.* She saw it now, as clearly as if it were mapped out before her. The only option still left open.

"We'll have to find a landline someplace," she said, swallowing her grief, "contact the sheriff, and get him to send out cars and helicopters, whatever he can, before it's too— Wait. What's that up ahead?"

She stared in wonder at a pair of round lights, wreathed in smoke, one disk above the other. Beside it was a flashing red-and-white bar, also vertical.

"Car crash," Cole said, coaxing a bit more speed from his shuddering pickup.

As soon as he spoke, her brain made sense of what she was seeing: the steaming wreckage of a sheriff's car lying on its side, the slow pulse of its light bar like a beating heart.

"TRACE. WAKE up, Trace. Please talk to me."

Trace didn't want to wake up, not with his head pounding as if he'd gulped a fifth of vodka and his nose so stopped up, he was gasping through his mouth. But the frantic note in his wife's voice convinced him that whatever she wanted, it was urgent. Besides, something wet was hitting his face, an annoying drip that had him turning his head to avoid it and forcing his eyes open.

What the hell was going on?

At the sight of Jill dangling from the car's seat just above him, it all came rushing back. The dark shape shooting out of nowhere, headlights off and automatic gunfire blazing. The impact as it rammed them, pushing the cruiser off the road.

And somewhere in the background, the bitter taste of disappointment at the fact that it had been his *ex* and not his *wife* calling his name.

"I just radioed. Help's coming," Jill said as she fought to unlatch her seat belt.

A glimpse of white—the deployed side air bag that was now hanging limp above her—reminded him that her door had taken the full force of the impact before their cruiser's wheels left the pavement.

"Hurt?" he tried to ask her, but the word came out a grunt.

Apparently she understood him anyway. "I'm okay," she told him, though even in this dim light he could see that her lip was bleeding. Dripping onto his face, which felt soaked already.

But then, he thought with a flash of irritation, Jill had always hated admitting she was sick or injured, had always stubbornly refused to give in to what she considered a sign of weakness. Apparently neither the beating Jimmy James Barlow had dished out, nor the miscarriage that followed had changed that about her. So why should he imagine a little thing like a major crash would do the trick?

Disentangling herself from her shoulder harness, she crawled down into the backseat behind him, then reached over it to squeeze his hand. "What about you, Trace? How bad is it? Do you want me to help you out of your belt?"

More than anything, he wanted to tell her that he was fine, too, wanted to ease the worry he heard in her voice. But for him, personal integrity had always meant a lot more than machismo, and that meant being honest with himself as well as others.

Besides, he had seen enough wrecks and attended enough first responder training sessions during his years with the department to know a thing or two about potential outcomes. And if Jill acted on impulse and emotion, and tried to move him instead of waiting for EMS to show up with their backboards and neck braces, things could get a whole lot worse than he sensed they were already.

"I'm not sure, hon," he finally said, reverting to his pet name to blunt the answer to her question. "My head hurts pretty bad, but I'm more worried by what doesn't. I can't feel a damned thing below my chest."

Chapter Ten

Colonel Drew Woodsen's voice came through Cole's cell phone like a buzz saw as his former commanding officer chewed through the same message he'd been trying to get across for the past three days, ever since Cole's return to town with Lisa. "I know you're a civilian now, but you're worrying me, Sawyer. Get it through your thick head that you're in no way responsible for anything to do with Staff Sergeant Meador's family. And do it before you wreck your life."

"No disrespect, sir, but you're no longer my C.O.," Cole growled as he pulled his rental car to a stop in front of the modest but well-kept older two-story where Lisa lived. His heart pounded as he stared at her front doorstep. This time, no matter what, he would not be turned away.

"I'm your friend still, whether or not you know it," Woodsen told him. "The FBI and the sheriff's department will do everything they can to find this missing kid. They don't need some ex-commando working off a nonexistent debt by mucking around in their business, and Lisa Meador certainly doesn't need you unburdening your soul while she's worried half to death about her—"

"I have to go, sir," Cole lied, pressing a random phone key. "That's my lawyer calling, and he charges by the millisecond."

"Probably calling to remind you that your U.S. Marshal's career will be over before it starts if you don't stay the hell out of—"

Cole disconnected, then blew out a deep breath. It was true that his attorney, too, had advised him to walk away from this mess. But neither he nor Drew had to live with the memory of the suicide bomber's final, desperate look, or the concussion that followed as the Afghan shoppers and a single American serviceman were torn to pieces in the blast that followed the detonation.

And neither of them had witnessed the look on Lisa's face when a pair of kidnappers made off with her only child. Neither of them had tasted the sweetness of her kiss or held her in his arms the way he had.

"Hell with it," Cole told himself as he climbed out of the sedan he was driving while his truck was in the shop. Sure, it might be smarter to let the authorities worry about finding her son, and let the lawyer he had hired focus on clearing his own name as soon as possible. But just as dangerous military missions quickly forged bonds between soldiers, the hours he had shared with her had left him feeling a connection he could not ignore.

A connection that would be broken, irredeemably betrayed, the moment she found out that he had watched her husband's death without doing a thing to try to stop it.

Still, he couldn't stop himself from knocking at her door, where the only response was Rowdy's barking. He pounded again, hard enough that the autumn wreath that hung there jumped with the impact. At its center was a peephole, where the older man who had turned him away earlier—Lisa's father, he assumed—could look out. The man was probably standing there now, cursing his unwelcome return.

Inside, a chain rattled and the dead bolt disengaged. As

the door opened, Cole steeled himself to argue his way past Lisa's gatekeeper.

But this morning it wasn't the gruff-looking man who had identified himself as a retired cop in an attempt to buy himself authority. Instead, Lisa herself answered, the hands that cradled Rowdy trembling as she studied him with reddened eyes.

"Lisa..." During more than a decade of military service, Cole had witnessed so much human suffering that he'd hardened himself against it, forming a tough shell so he could function. But just as it had three days before, Lisa's pain sliced through his warrior's defenses, cutting straight to the beating heart beneath.

"Come on in—and hurry," she said, staring past his shoulder. "There are reporters right behind you. Vultures."

As she ducked out of sight, Cole turned to look, wondering where on earth the press had hidden their vehicles. Aggravated that he hadn't spotted them, he glared at an attractive redhead named Penny Carlson whom he recognized from one of the Austin network affiliates.

In an instant the shrewd hunger in her eyes changed to a look of made-for-TV sympathy as her cameraman moved into position to capture the exchange. Great, Cole thought. Just what he needed: video evidence that he'd allowed his need to check on Lisa to overwhelm his better judgment, along with his C.O.'s and attorney's sensible advice.

"I'm so sorry for Mrs. Meador's tragic situation," the reporter told him gravely. "Please convey our sympathies, and tell her that if she'd like to try to get a message to the kidnappers, I would be happy to set up another on-camera plea for his return."

"Would you like to be arrested for trespassing?" He let the business card she tried to hand him flutter to a doormat that read *Welcome, Friends!* "Because I'm pretty sure you've been told to stay off the property. And I'm absolutely positive the sheriff's department would be glad for an excuse to toss you in the county lockup after your last report."

He was guessing on both counts, partly because of this particular reporter's on-air speculation regarding the Tuller County deputy who'd been airlifted to an Austin trauma center. Cole had known from the first moment he'd glimpsed the terrified female deputy who'd flagged them down that her partner's injuries were serious, most likely life-threatening. He wondered who had leaked it to the reporter that the pair had once been man and wife. And why the hell this woman had decided their personal history was anybody's business but their own.

"Please," said the reporter, "I only want to help bring Tyler home."

Her expression was so sincere that Cole might have believed it—if she hadn't first glanced into the camera before delivering her plea. Shaking his head in disgust, he picked up her card and tore it into pieces. "If you're so concerned, then get out there and find him, instead of exploiting people's tragedies for ratings."

As the torn bits fluttered toward the front step, he ducked inside the house, hoping like hell that Penny's vanity would prevent her from using that unflattering bit of footage.

Lisa locked the door behind him, her smile barely touching the pain in her damp eyes.

"Thank you for that," she said, tugging at the edges of a gray sweater she had thrown on over a black V-neck tee and faded jeans that hugged her curves in ways he had no business noticing. "I've been wanting to tell those people off for days. Actually, I've been wanting to hurl pots of boiling oil from the upstairs windows, but my father wouldn't let me."

He smiled at her gallows humor, understanding all too well that it might be the only thing holding her together. But she was already turning from him, her hand shaking as she pinched the bridge of her nose. "You must think I'm horrible, joking when my son's out there somewhere, scared and—"

Before Cole could stop to think, he was gathering her in his arms as she disintegrated into weeping. Feeling more useless than ever, he rubbed her back and tried to think of what to say to make things better. But he was no better at soothing her tears than he had been at getting back her child.

With the thought, the recriminations that had been keeping him up at night came crashing in on him. He swallowed past a painful lump, thinking of how no real Ranger would have allowed the darkness and a single AK-47 to stop him from taking out one woman. How not one of the men he had commanded would have allowed her or her accomplice to escape alive, much less take the child with them and go on to attack two deputies in their patrol car.

But then, if he'd been a decent Ranger in the first place, she wouldn't be facing this crisis without Tyler's father.

A creak from the staircase warned him of another presence a moment before a familiar scowl appeared. "Damn it, boy. How many times do I need to tell you? Lisa doesn't need any more gawkers coming in here to upset her."

Pulling free of his embrace, Lisa shook her head, her face flushing. "No, Dad. This is Cole, the Ranger who risked his life trying to get Tyler back."

"*Ex*-Ranger," Cole corrected, touched that, for all she'd

been through, she would care enough to come to his defense.

Her father ran a hand over his gray brush cut and speared Cole with a look of pure contempt. "Bang-up job you did there, boy, shooting my daughter and letting the kidnappers go free."

"It might not've been my finest moment, but let's get one thing straight between us," Cole said, in no mood for the man's attitude. "You can call me Cole or Sawyer, but I don't answer to 'boy.'"

The ex-cop gaped in surprise, then nodded.

"Come on, Dad," Lisa said. "Cole was hurt helping me." She gestured to the small bandage covering the blistered skin on his forearm.

"It's no big deal," he told her.

Her father's hard stare never budged. "You say you're an ex-Ranger. So, what do you do now, bo—*Sawyer?*"

"Keep myself in shape and stay busy doing volunteer work until the next class of U.S. Marshals starts in two months. I've been accepted. Or at least I *was* accepted before your daughter walked into that bank. Still waiting to see if I'll be cleared to attend."

"Oh, Cole…" Lisa gave her father another look until he offered Cole his hand.

"Sid Hartfield," he said by way of introduction.

Shaking hands, Cole said, "Pleased to meet you, sir. With those reporters swarming, I'm sure Lisa's glad for your help."

"He ran off Penny Carlson," Lisa told her father in an apparent attempt to ease the tension.

"She came back again? Brave girl. As well as a damned nuisance."

"You know, Dad, since Cole's here, maybe now would be a good time for you to go pick up those groceries."

"I was just putting away all those cakes and casseroles the neighbor ladies dropped off. Still don't understand why they thought they had to bring enough to feed an army."

"That's just their way of showing that they care. Let me take care of the food while you go."

"If you're really that desperate to get rid of me..." her father grumbled, then abruptly brightened. "There's always the chance that I could back over a couple of reporters on my way out." Swinging a look toward Cole, he added, "You *can* stay with her for a half hour, can't you?"

Cole nodded. "Take as long as you need."

Hartfield bobbed his head, then grabbed a light jacket and an old-fashioned beige porkpie hat off a coatrack by the door. After kissing Lisa's cheek, he told her, "If this one gives you any trouble or decides he's got better things to do, you call me, and I'll be back here before you can spit."

"Don't forget more tissues. And we're low on dog food, too," Lisa told him, ticking off the items on her fingers.

She waited until he left to speak again. "Finally. I'm really sorry about my dad. He means well, and I love him to pieces, but there are times..."

"Under the circumstances," Cole said diplomatically, "it's no wonder he's being so protective."

"Embarrassing is what he's being." She shook her head. "And he wonders why I refused to move back home after Devin..."

"At least you know you have a father who loves you." It was more than he could say for his. Oh, the old man had been proud—at least according to Cole's mother—when his only son had made it through the grueling Ranger training and started accumulating medals and promotions. It simply wasn't his father's way, his mom said, excusing her husband as she did so often, to "make a big fuss over these things." Which was pretty ironic, considering the size of the fuss he'd made when Cole had left the military.

"He's only trying to protect you," he told Lisa.

"He's just afraid I'm going to take off looking for Tyler the second his back is turned," she said.

"Are you?"

When she didn't answer, he wondered if she knew something the investigators didn't. From what little he had heard on the news, he'd gotten the impression they had completely lost track of the kidnappers. And Texas was one hell of a huge haystack to search, especially if Evie and her partner had managed to switch vehicles again. Not to mention the possibility that they'd left the state, or even crossed the border into Mexico. "Do you have any idea where they might be? Have you remembered something? Has someone contacted you, Lisa?"

She shook her head. "No one has, not yet, but I know it could still happen, no matter what the sheriff thinks. But there is one thing that I'm sure of. My son is still alive and waiting for me, and I *will* bring him home."

He wanted to ask how she knew, but her expression answered for her. Though he suspected it was no more than a psychological defense against unbearable pain, he didn't have it in him to question her faith in mother's intuition. Besides, he would rather face this determination—or a nest of enemy snipers—than deal with another round of tears.

He followed her into the kitchen, done in blue-and-white tile. Bowls, plastic-wrapped plates and bakery boxes, many with open cards beside them, covered almost every inch of counter space. There were several flower arrangements, but his eyes were drawn to a crystal vase in the center of the table, filled with sunny yellow irises.

"Thank you for those," she said, nodding toward them. "That was really thoughtful. And I especially appreciate that you picked something that didn't make me think of funerals."

"The woman at the flower shop told me these stand for hope," he said, feeling a rush of embarrassment at the amount of thought he'd put into what should have been a simple gesture.

"Coffee?" Lisa asked, indicating a nearly full pot. "Dad just made it. And there's a plate of cinnamon rolls in here somewhere, if you'd like something—"

"I didn't come to eat your food and drink your coffee."

"Then why *are* you here?" She shrugged. "Honestly, I wouldn't blame you one bit for wanting to put all this behind you and forget it."

"In case you haven't noticed, I'm not the cut-and-run type, and I sure wasn't gonna be put off by your dad's attempts to get rid of me. I needed to see how you are, and I have a right to know what's happening with the investigation. No one will tell me a damned thing."

Including whether he would officially be cleared of any wrongdoing, a factor that was crucial if he were to have any hope of becoming a U.S. Marshal. But as much as he tried to convince himself that a rational self-interest was his main reason for returning, he knew damned well that the secret that he carried was just as big a factor.

She turned from the refrigerator, where she'd just found room for a covered casserole dish. "Wait a minute. You came earlier?"

He nodded. "I tried to explain to your dad that I wasn't a reporter in disguise or some true-crime freak out for juicy details, but—"

"Sorry about that. But as far as the investigation goes..." She peeked inside one of the boxes, then closed it after pulling out another envelope. "I doubt I know any more than you do. The sheriff and the FBI have been a lot better at asking questions than sharing information.

"For all I know," she added as she opened the envelope, "they still consider me a suspect, too."

"That's ridiculous," he said, before reminding himself that initially he had thought the same thing.

"Well, thanks for the vote of confidence," she said, as Rowdy balanced on his hind legs, begging for a handout. "Maybe we can vouch for each other. But then they'd probably decide we're in cahoots or something. No one's come right out and said so, but I've been asked a dozen times for my 'version of events.'"

"They've been asking me a lot of questions, too. My lawyer's advised me to steer clear of further involvement just in case they decide to come after me for drawing my gun and—"

Lisa tossed the dog the corner of a sugar cookie. "Then maybe you shouldn't come back. Seriously, I don't want you getting into trouble, not after you risked your life to try to help me. Which reminds me, are you really all right?"

"I am," he said, glad that the bruised hip and burned arm were both healing so well. "How's *your* arm?"

"Believe me, a few stitches and a mild concussion are the least of my worries." Her dismissive expression turned to a frown. "Listen, Cole, I've told the investigators you were innocent. I swore I talked you into helping me chase down the kidnappers."

Her concern touched him, considering everything she'd been through. True, she had pulled a gun on him—twice—but only under extreme duress. The real Lisa Meador seemed as thoughtful as she was beautiful, even in her current state.

"I'll get it sorted out, but right now," he said honestly, "I'm a lot more worried about you and your family."

Earlier, he'd tried to convince himself that once he'd checked on her and learned what he could, he would walk away as he'd been advised. But meeting her in her moment of crisis, seeing her passion and her courage, had reawakened something in him, even if it was only the dim hope of redemption.

Her hand trembling, she tucked a loose lock of wavy brown hair behind her ear and pulled a flowered "Thinking of You" card from its envelope, then scanned the message inside. Her throat bobbed with a hard swallow, her eyes filling with tears.

"I do have a little good news," he added, eager to pull her from the brink. "I understand the teller from the bank had a healthy baby."

"A b-baby boy." She flipped the card closed abruptly. "I—I was so glad to hear it."

Despite her claim, her face went chalk-white, and Cole cursed himself for bringing up a child—any child—while hers was missing and in danger. How was it he always managed to say the wrong thing?

"I'm sorry," he said.

"No, it's me, and I really am h-happy for that woman, especially after I scared her the w-way I did." She gave her eyes an angry swipe. "Oh, damn it. Could you please grab me a couple of tissues? I think there are still a few in the powder room by the back door."

She pointed him in the right direction, and he hurried to retrieve the box, happy to be given something to do.

"Here you go," he said, as he returned to find her looking more stricken than ever as she wiped what looked like white icing from her shaking fingers with a paper towel.

"Thanks. You can set them down anywhere." She

closed the cake box and turned her back to him quickly. "I'm okay for now."

Though he thought it was odd that she would send him for tissues she didn't need, he was grateful she was feeling better. Vowing to avoid upsetting her again, he decided that sharing more positive news would help, especially since it didn't involve a child. "I understand it looks as though the security guard is going to pull through."

Lisa nodded. "That's great. I heard the same thing from Deputy Keller at the station—the one whose partner was hurt so badly. Poor woman looked as if she hadn't slept in days."

"Did she mention Deputy Sutherland's condition?"

Turning from the counter, Lisa hugged her middle. "Even if he survives," she said, her brown eyes somber, "he could be permanently paralyzed."

"Such a damned waste," Cole said, stricken by how quickly and cruelly a person's life could change forever. Just as Lisa's had done when a pair of carjackers took her son.

Changing the subject, he asked, "Were you able to remember any more about Evie LeStrange?"

"Nothing. Nothing at all. You know, I really don't…" Her hand jerked to her forehead, where she massaged the pressure points. "I'm glad you stopped by, Cole. Thank you. But I think it would be better if you left now."

Troubled by her abrupt shift of behavior, he asked, "What's wrong, Lisa?" Had his mention of Evie been the trigger? Or was she still thinking of the teller, with her husband at her side and her healthy baby boy in her arms?

"What *isn't?*" she asked, her voice breaking and fresh moisture gleaming along her lower lashes. "I have an awful headache, I'm not sleeping and my stomach hurts because the only thing I've been able to cram down are these stupid brownies." She picked up a paper plate and flung the chocolate squares into the trash can.

"Is there anything I can do? Anything I can get you?"

She snatched up a handful of tissues and shoved them into the lumpy pocket of her sweater. "If you'll just leave, I can go to bed and lie down."

No way was he abandoning her in this state. There was something going on here, something more than she was saying. "I can't do that, Lisa. I promised your father I would stay till he gets back. And that's what I'm going to do. But you can head upstairs and rest if you'd like."

Maybe she just needed to cry again and didn't want him to see her doing it. That must be it.

She hesitated, their gazes locking, and he was sure she was about to throw herself into his arms again. As useless as he had been at consoling her the first time, he could hardly blame her when she turned around and bolted for the stairs.

WITH THE RESTLESS ENERGY of a caged lioness, Lisa paced the confines of her bedroom. Why couldn't Cole just leave as she had asked him? She needed the ex-Ranger, with his talent for interference, out of here before her dad returned.

With a trembling sigh, she reached into her pocket, past the camouflaging tissues, and pulled out the first of the two items she had shoved in when she sent him out of the room: the card left with the cake she'd found on her doorstep earlier.

Since the box had been stamped with the name of a local bakery, she had thought nothing of the fact that the offering wasn't homemade. She'd been equally unsurprised by the innocuous greeting on the card's front, a supportive message little different from dozens of other cards she had received.

But there the resemblance ended, because a single glance inside was enough to send her pulse racing. This, she'd realized instantly, was the communication she'd been waiting for, and it hadn't come in a phone call that the FBI would hear through their tap, or through the mail, which was also being strictly monitored. Instead, the message had arrived through a local delivery, one that Evie must somehow have arranged.

Opening the card once again, Lisa stared at the enclosed picture, which looked like a low-res camera photo. Though the image was of poor quality, she could easily make out Tyler in his booster seat, looking as if he might burst into tears at any moment. He was holding up a national newspaper with yesterday's headlines; she recognized the lead story right away.

"I'm coming, baby, I promise," she whispered as her own tears dripped onto the picture. "Just a tiny bit longer, my brave little soldier. I know you can do this."

Forcing herself to turn it over, she reread the handwritten message she had only skimmed before.

There were only a few lines, words so blunt, so cruel, that the very sight of them had hot bile burning her throat. Fighting to keep herself from hyperventilating, she forced herself to focus not on the threat but on the demand for a private meeting a half hour after midnight. A meeting she had no idea how she could possibly pull off with no car, no privacy and an all-too-capable babysitter close at hand.

"Where, Evie? Where do you want me to go?" Would the second item contain the answer, a cheap prepaid cell phone hidden, as the card had promised, under the cake itself?

Pulling it out of an icing-spotted plastic sandwich bag, she switched on the power button. As she waited for it to find a signal, her gaze flicked to the glowing numbers of the digital clock on her nightstand. Numbers counting down the hours and the minutes she had left.

Left to live, she realized, well aware of the import of Evie's cruel message: that Lisa's sole chance to save Tyler was in exchanging her own life for her son's.

Swallowing past a lump in her throat, she told herself that if that was what the sadistic bitch demanded, it was what she was prepared to offer.

Unless she could somehow manage to kill Evie LeStrange first.

Chapter Eleven

"No, I won't go home," Deputy Jill Keller argued with her boss. Exhausted and emotionally wrung out, she felt the burning threat of tears, but she would be damned if she would shed a single one in front of Sheriff Hank Stewart, or any place where her coworkers or, worse yet, those FBI outsiders might see.

Stewart hauled his considerable bulk out of his desk chair. "You're not thinking like an investigator right now. You're thinking like a wife—a wife who needs to be by Trace's side."

"I. Am. Not. His. Wife," she ground out through clenched teeth. "And just in case you or anybody else around here has forgotten that, believe me, the point was driven home when I showed up at the hospital in Austin. I'm no longer next of kin. No longer anything to him." Her vision began to blur. "Damn it all."

She whirled, turning her back and wiping away the angry tears. "I'm sorry, sir. It's just— I'm tired."

The floor creaked with Stewart's footsteps as he came up behind her, then patted her back with a meaty hand. Could this day get any more humiliating?

"Don't apologize for being human," he said, his deep voice softer than she had ever heard it. "It's been an emotional time for everybody around here. You know I hired that boy practically right outta high school. Taught him everything I know. Nobody could've ever asked for a better deputy, a better man than—hell, girl, now you've got me—"

It was his turn to pull away, fumbling in embarrassment for the folded bandanna in his pocket. "If I was any kind of a gentleman, I'd offer this to you," he said before blowing his nose into it with a honk so loud it made them both laugh.

"No, thanks," she said. "I'd just as soon you keep it. But keep me on the task force, too. If I can't be part of Trace's recovery—and believe me, his parents have made it quite plain that's not my place—I have to be a part of hunting down the bastards who did this to him."

Stewart shook his head. "Sorry, Jill, but you know those FBI boys already figure we're just a bunch of ignorant country yokels out here. I won't have 'em believin' we're so unprofessional as to let some trigger-happy deputy with a personal involvement jeopardize the investigation."

"Who says I'm trigger-happy?"

"How 'bout that witness from the bank parking lot, for starters? The one you pulled your gun on."

"But he was being deliberately uncooperative."

Stewart rolled his eyes. "When it comes to getting the job done, you've always been a hard-driving, take-no-prisoners kind of gal. It's something I like about you, even when it gives me a damned headache. But in this particular case, I don't need some college boy special agent from the bureau tellin' me that you've lost all perspective. I can see it in your face, girl. Now get on out of here for a few days, leastwise till we catch those sons of bitches."

"You don't understand. I *need* this."

"And I need you to go home, or, better yet, drive back

to Austin and try to make peace with your former in-laws. Because you're the one Trace needs by his side, the face he wants to see when he wakes up. You mark my words, that boy's no more moved on in the past year than you have."

The ever-present anger flared, flashing red as blood across her vision. "With all due respect, sir," she managed, "what's between Trace and me is none of your damned business."

Their gazes locked, and she saw the heat building behind his, the struggle as he fought to control his temper. *That makes two of us.*

"You're right about that, Deputy," he finally told her. "What *is* my business is your job performance, and right now you're not fit for duty."

"I can be. I swear to you, I'll—"

"This subject isn't open for discussion," he said sternly. "My only question is, are you gonna take a few days willingly, or do I need to confiscate your badge and gun?"

Jaw set, she glared straight at him before unpinning her badge and unbuckling her holster.

"You can take this badge and gun and—" she started.

"Before you finish that sentence," he said, his round face florid, "you might want to think about what that hot head of yours is about to cost you, Deputy. Or maybe I should say 'what *else*,' because it seems to me like it's already cost you something a hell of a lot more important than any job on earth."

Jill opened her mouth, still ready to tell him what he could do with his job. But an image of Trace lying in intensive care, his face pale and his body the center of a beeping spider's web of tubes and wires, rose before her, the single glimpse she'd managed before his mother shrieked, "Are you happy now, Jill? Happy that you've finally finished off what breaking his heart started? Because I know this is all your fault. There's absolutely no doubt in my mind."

Releasing a deep breath, she looked into Stewart's eyes and nodded. "I—I'll be taking some vacation, Sheriff. You have my cell number if you need me."

She quickly left the office. But not before replacing the badge and rebuckling the gun holster that were as much a part of her as any of her limbs.

WITH THE SAME RUTHLESS efficiency he had once used to fieldstrip an automatic weapon or plan a stealth mission, Cole organized the excess of food gifts in the kitchen. But as he found refrigerator space for the perishables, moved all the baked goods to one countertop and trashed anything that no longer appeared edible, his mind kept wandering to Lisa and the way she'd so abruptly tried to dismiss him.

It was probably no more than he'd thought earlier, a stressed, exhausted woman wanting the privacy to break down, but something about her behavior troubled him, especially when he checked the box she had been looking into and found the cake inside tipped over and all but destroyed.

Could Lisa have done that, he asked himself, recalling her wiping icing off her hand, and if so, why? Wondering if there might have been something disturbing in the message that came with it—perhaps another interview request from the relentless Penny Carlson—he began looking for the accompanying card he'd seen Lisa reading.

He couldn't find it anywhere, not among the other cards, on the floor or in the trash can. Had she taken it upstairs with her for some reason? And could that card be the reason for her sudden eagerness to be rid of him?

Cole stiffened, a buzz arcing across millions of nerve endings. He could be dead wrong, but he would rather make a fool of himself and get kicked out of her house forever than take a chance on letting her do something desperate on her own.

He hadn't made it two steps when the side door off the kitchen opened.

"Hey, Sawyer, how 'bout a hand here?" asked Lisa's father, who was juggling sacks of groceries and a bag of dog food that a little bit of fluff like Rowdy couldn't finish in months.

"We have to hurry." Grabbing the kibble, Cole slung the bag onto the counter. "We need to check on Lisa right now."

Instantly alarmed, the old man dropped the other groceries next to the dog food. "I thought you said you'd keep an eye on her. Where is she?"

Heading for the stairs, Cole explained, "She told me she felt sick and she was going up to lie down. But I just realized she took something up there with her—a card that I'm pretty sure upset her."

Sid Hartfield was right behind him, saying, "Hold your horses. You should let me—"

But Cole was already halfway up the staircase, and he wasn't stopping now. "Which door?" he called back.

"What?" Struggling to catch up, Sid Hartfield was panting up the steps behind Cole.

"Which one is her bedroom?"

"First door on the left, but you be sure and knock," her father said.

Cole tapped once to humor him before flinging the door open. "Lisa?"

He saw no one except Rowdy, who was wagging his tail, and beyond him, only a dresser and a neatly made four-poster bed, with a closed laptop sitting beside it on the nightstand. Undisturbed, a pair of curtains partly obscured a closed window. Noticing what appeared to be an open walk-in closet, Cole strode toward it and called her name again.

But there was no one there, either.

From the hall, her father called, "Bathroom door's closed." He pounded on it. "Lisa? You in the shower?"

As Cole approached, he heard the water running.

"Maybe she can't hear me," said her father.

Bypassing him, Cole tried the door. Locked. More concerned than ever, he pounded on the door so hard that it shook on its frame. "Turn off the water," he shouted, his voice a loud, deep rumble that the neighbors probably heard. "Lisa, it's important."

When there was no response, he added the one lie sure to get through to her, no matter how much she craved privacy. "The sheriff's here to see you."

Catching on, her father added, "About Tyler."

As the tension in the hallway built, the water continued running. Glancing at Lisa's father, Cole said, "This door is coming down."

Without waiting for an answer, he backed up and took a run at it, then kicked hard. There was a splintering crack, but the doors in the old house were solid, and it took two more bruising charges before he had it off its hinges.

Squeezed into the bathroom, he saw that Lisa wasn't in the shower, and the steam in the room wasn't nearly as thick as he might have expected—because the window was wide open. A window that he quickly discovered was only a few feet above the roof of the back porch. From there, it would be an easy climb down to the backyard and the escape that she had been so desperate to achieve.

As she climbed into her Honda and started for home, Jill Keller was fuming, still thinking of Sheriff Stewart's last words to her. So he, like everybody else, blamed her for the breakup of her marriage. No surprise there, but she wondered, would Stewart, whose own wife had left him years ago citing the complaint that he was never home, put up with the kind of ultimatum Trace had given her?

"If you really want a family, you're going to have to find another career," he'd said, while she was still reeling in the wake of the beating and the miscarriage that followed, her soul ravaged with guilt that went far deeper than the pain of her physical injuries.

It was a guilt magnified a hundredfold by the knowledge that Trace blamed her, too, for pushing the boundaries as she always did, mercilessly harassing Jimmy James Barlow, a man she absolutely *knew* was regularly knocking the snot out of his live-in girlfriend. When she'd finally badgered the girlfriend into filing charges and shown up to arrest him, Jill had made a point of forcing the bastard to do the perp walk in front of his drinking buddies, and yeah, she'd lobbed a few humiliating zingers his way, but no more than a worm like that had coming.

But the beaten-down girlfriend soon lost her nerve, resulting in Barlow's release the next morning. Furious, he'd broken her jaw before lying in wait for Jill, who'd been off-duty and unarmed, on her way home from a visit to the obstetrician, when he'd beaten her until the heartbeat she had just heard for the first time was irrevocably silenced.

"I can't go through this again," Trace had told her, tears gleaming in his dark eyes. *"I won't risk losing you— or leaving any kids we might have motherless."*

But law enforcement wasn't only what Jill did; it was who she was. It was all she could remember ever wanting since first watching her father, a former Tuller County sheriff, pin on his own badge and strap on his leather holster. His heart had given out when she was twelve, but she preferred to remember him standing tall in uniform, a tough-talking, hard-driving scourge on the area's law-breakers.

Certainly he wouldn't have wasted a moment worrying whether he'd hurt the feelings of a piece of garbage like Jimmy James Barlow, who was now serving a long sentence.

But this morning it wasn't her father's once hale and hearty image that rose from the grave to haunt her. It was the thought of Trace, lying near death in that hospital in Austin. Lying there because of the murderous actions of a pair of carjackers—the same carjackers who had stolen Lisa Meador's five-year-old son.

Low in Jill's belly, a spark of rage reignited. Because anger was an old friend, far more comfortable than grief.

It was that anger that had her turning off her normal route with the thought of questioning Lisa Meador one more time. Distracted by her personal tragedy, the woman would neither know nor care that Jill was supposed to be on leave.

Just down the street from Lisa's house, Jill stopped short, unable to believe what she was seeing. But sure enough, it was Lisa Meador, looking around nervously as she wheeled a bicycle from her backyard toward the street.

Was she looking to see if the coast was clear of reporters so she could stretch her legs and get a little fresh air? No, that couldn't be it. She kept looking back at the house, not the street, and everything about her body language communicated furtiveness.

What the hell was going on?

Only one way to find out, Jill decided, her law enforcement instincts prickling with anticipation. On leave or not, she was damned well going to tail the woman. Because she would bet her badge that whatever Lisa was sneaking off to do, it had nothing to do with exercise.

THOUGH THE MORNING WAS cool, Lisa grew warm as she pedaled down the side streets at top speed. With every bump, her upper arm throbbed and her headache pounded harder, but she didn't dare slow down. Besides, the pain of her healing injuries was nothing compared to her guilt. It was bad enough she'd lied to Cole, a man who'd come to see her when he had every reason to run the other way, but leaving as she had done would scare her dad out of his mind.

As brave a face as he'd been putting on for her sake, she knew it was already everything he could do to deal with the disappearance of his only grandchild. With her mother lost years before to cancer and Devin gone, too, she and Tyler were all the family he had left. Though he sometimes drove her crazy, she could barely stand the thought of hurting him this way.

"I'll bring Tyler home, I swear it," she murmured, still wondering how, exactly, she could force Evie to keep her word.

At least Lisa had come up with a plan to get to the meeting place whose location Evie had texted to her cell phone, a plan that didn't include bicycling across Texas. Even by car, it was going to be a long trip, a good eight and a half to nine hours if she drove straight through. She had briefly considered flying but quickly learned that it would actually take longer, once she factored in that the nearest airport to the remote, mountainous Big Bend region would still put her another four hours away by car. At least Evie had tossed her wallet into the straw bag with the gun, so she had her license and credit cards.

As she stood at the car rental counter ten minutes later, she prayed the rental agent hadn't seen her pleading for her son's return on the news. What she needed was a distraction, something to prevent the woman from realizing who she was and tipping off the press—or the cops. After a few desperate moments, inspiration struck. As she handed her license to the young woman behind the counter, she gave in to the tears that were never far from the surface.

"Is something wrong, miss?" From behind the woman's glasses, blue eyes flicked up from the ID. "Ms. Meador?"

Lisa wiped her hands over her sore eyes. "I—I'm in a hurry. I'm terrified my boyfriend's going to find me." She shook her head, silently praying for forgiveness. "The last time I tried to get clear of him, he put me in the hospital."

The agent's hand flew to cover a small gasp. "Oh, my goodness. Well, I can certainly hurry things up on your rental."

"If he comes by, could you please keep it to yourself I've been here?" asked Lisa. "You'll recognize him right away. He's good-looking, really tall and built. He has short light brown hair, and he can be very charming when it suits him."

"As a matter of policy," the woman told her, her eyes sympathetic, "we never give out our customers' personal information. But I'll definitely be watching out for this guy. He sounds really dangerous."

"Believe me, I have the bruises to prove it." Feeling like the worst sort of fraud, Lisa touched the woman's hand as she took back the license. "Thank you so much for your help. I can't tell you what this means to me."

If it meant saving her son, it would be worth whatever lies she had to resort to, even slandering a man as undeserving, as heroic, as Cole Sawyer.

"SHE REALLY DID it," Sid Hartfield said. "She's somehow got it in her head that she can go out and find Tyler. How she thinks she's going to manage, I can't imagine, when the sheriff's department and the FBI haven't so far."

"Maybe there was something in that card that gave her an idea where they're hiding," Cole said.

"Then why wouldn't she tell one of us, or dial 9-1-1, instead of sneaking out like some teenager?"

Cole shook his head. "Threats, maybe? I can't tell you, but I do know one thing. Wherever Lisa's heading, she's not getting there on foot, so we should check nearby rental lots."

"I'm calling the sheriff right now," Hartfield said. "Or maybe even those high and mighty federal boys they sent out."

"I think you should, but in the meantime, I'll head out and start looking in case I can catch her," Cole suggested.

Her father frowned, his forehead wrinkling. "I'd rather go myself, but it's always possible she'll come back or at least call home, so I should probably be here in case. It's not like her to let me worry. Not like her at all."

Unless Cole missed his guess, neither was escaping through a second-story window. "Does she have a cell phone on her?"

Hartfield shook his head. "She hasn't replaced the one the kidnappers took yet. We think it was destroyed, since the cell phone company can't pin down the location through the GPS. But she still might call from wherever she's gone."

Cole nodded. "Let's exchange numbers. Then I'm out of here."

Raking his hands through his steel-gray brush cut, Sid said, "Just promise me one thing, boy. Swear to me you won't screw things up again."

Cole was on the road in minutes, wishing like hell he could have given the older man what he most craved: a guarantee that he would save Lisa and her son. But Cole hadn't made that promise, couldn't, for he knew all too well that anything might happen, from Lisa changing her mind and returning to apologize, to her murder as she charged into some sort of ransom exchange scenario gone wrong.

As he thought about the latter possibility, he wondered if the kidnappers could know enough about her to realize she had likely received a good-size payout from the life insurance policy nearly every combat soldier opted to take. Though it was possible, her modest home, older car and strictly middle-class job made her an unlikely candidate to catch the attention of a criminal looking for a big score.

Still racking his brain over why her son had been taken, Cole pulled through an open gate and into the only car rental agency within a reasonable walking distance of Lisa's home. Like nearly everything in Coopersville, this business was small, consisting only of a mostly empty lot surrounded by a chain-link fence, with a hutlike structure at its center and a shed off in the corner, where a uniformed employee was hosing off a hatchback.

Spotting no one else, he walked into the office, where a young woman in thick, tortoiseshell glasses was furiously pecking away at a computer with two fingers.

His first impulse was to blurt out his questions and demand swift answers, but he reminded himself that this was no war zone, even if his need to find Lisa felt as urgent. Deciding on another tack, he pasted on his smoothest smile. "Thought I was the only one who still typed like that, though you're a heck of a lot faster."

The rental agent looked up sharply, her round cheeks

blazing. "Sorry, sir," she said. "I didn't hear you come in. May I help you?"

"Pretty morning," he said casually, though inside, he was thrumming with impatience. "Been busy so far today?"

Eyes the color of worn denim met his, then flicked back down to her hands as her blush deepened. Painfully shy, he decided. Or did she think he was hitting on her?

"It's been really quiet," she said, her voice barely louder than a mouse's squeak. "Um, did you—uh—did you have a reservation?"

"So I'm your first customer?" he asked.

"Is there something I can help you with?"

Hearing the tension in her voice, he decided he needed to work on his smooth smile, or at least get better at hiding his impatience. "I was just trying to figure out if my girlfriend already took care of the rental for our vacation like she promised, or if I should go ahead and handle it."

As far as cover stories went, it wouldn't win him any awards, but he thought it sounded halfway plausible.

"Oh. That's it?" Despite the forced smile, she still sounded strangely nervous. "No. She definitely hasn't been here today." After a brief hesitation, she squeaked out, "Would you like to hear about our upgrade specials? I can offer you a midsize, or even one of our premium vehicles for only the price of—"

"Sorry to interrupt, but maybe I'll try calling her again in case she went somewhere else," he said, pulling out his phone. "Thanks for your help."

Feeling that there was something off about her behavior, he hurried back to his car. As he thought about any other place where Lisa might have gotten a vehicle, he wondered if he had it all wrong. Maybe she'd gone to a friend's to ask for help.

On the seat beside him, his cell phone started ringing. Praying it was Hartfield calling to let him know his daughter had come to her senses and returned, he glanced at the screen and swore when he saw the name of his attorney.

But Jeff Schulz, a retired army officer Cole had met while working on a Homes for Wounded Heroes project, couldn't possibly be calling to chew him out already.

"I'm in kind of a rush here, but what's up, Jeff?"

"What's up is I've scored you a chance to talk with the assistant director of the U.S. Marshals' Training Division," Jeff said quickly. "He's something of a hard-ass and was going to take you off the class list 'pending a complete investigation,' which is bureaucrat-speak for something that'll drag on until you're sorry you ever bothered with it. Fortunately, I talked him into meeting with you personally. The catch is, you have to go to Georgia, and you have to get there fast."

"How fast?"

"He'll see you Wednesday at two-thirty to discuss this. That's two days from now, Cole, and he's only doing that much because I'm an old college buddy of a good friend of his. Even then, I had to personally put up my left nut for collateral against the claim that you'll be worth the trouble. So be there, and be convincing."

"Roger that. I'll be there," Cole said, reminding himself that whatever it would cost to buy an airline ticket on such short notice, the chance of getting himself back on track would be worth every penny. "And thanks for vouching for me. You can tell your wife the family jewels are safe."

After taking a moment to jot down the address of the assistant director's office, Cole ended the call and put the car into Reverse. The only other business Lisa could have reached on foot in a reasonable time was a dealership about a half mile distant, though he didn't think she could have bought a car on the spot.

If she wasn't there, he would call her father for ideas. Or maybe, by that time, the team assigned to her case would have arrived to step in. They were far better qualified to hunt her down than he was.

Backing from his parking spot, Cole struggled to convince himself that with federal and local law enforcement working tirelessly, Lisa and her son would soon be home celebrating, and that somewhere in southern Georgia, he would be doing the same thing, his conscience clear in the knowledge that he'd done what he could.

But no matter how hard he tried, he couldn't quite make himself believe it, so when he caught sight of something odd near the fence line, he hit the brakes to study it more closely.

It was a bicycle, he realized, lying on its side. A woman's bike, he saw as he climbed out of the car to take a closer look. Could Lisa have ridden it here, then abandoned it once she rented a car? Could she have convinced the rental agent to lie for her?

A flutter of movement nearby attracted his attention, a loose scrap of paper kicked up by the breeze. A picture? He walked over to see what it was.

He stiffened at the sight of the frightened eyes staring out from the image. Tyler Meador's smudged, or maybe bruised, face, half-hidden behind the front page of yesterday's paper.

So he'd been right to be suspicious of the rental agent. Lisa *had* been here, and she must have accidentally dropped this in the parking lot when she claimed her rental. But there was no message on the page he'd picked up, which meant the instructions must have been written on the missing card.

His sense of urgency redoubled. It was imperative to stop Lisa before she left the area. If he walked away now, simply called 9-1-1 and told authorities what he knew, by the time they showed up she would be long gone—and walking into an ambush of the kidnappers' choosing on her own.

Making up his mind, he left the car and trotted toward the employee who was vacuuming out the vehicle he had been washing earlier. Because whatever Lisa had told the rental agent to keep her from cooperating, he would bet his bottom dollar she hadn't thought to talk to this guy, too, so he would at least have seen which direction she had taken.

Chapter Twelve

Sick with worry about Tyler and doubting every move she'd made, Lisa was still dimly aware of how lucky she had been to scoop up the rental lot's last SUV and get away so cleanly.

After swinging by the ATM, she'd made one final, high-risk stop. Things there had gone smoothly, too, allowing her to leave town without any trouble. Unfortunately, her route took her out on Sunset, toward the river, the same road she had traveled three days before with Cole behind the wheel.

Flashbacks flickered across her vision like jumbled still shots from a horror movie, sending her heart rate into overdrive. The pregnant teller's terrified face. Tyler's attempts to be brave as he'd clutched at Rowdy and his octopus. Evie LeStrange's hard glare before she'd slammed her gun into Lisa's head. The blur of Cole's dive as he'd fired at her.

Thinking back to Evie, her mind froze on the final image, zooming in on the angry sneer and blazing eyes that seemed almost too blue to be real.

What if they weren't? What if the color was as fake as the matching streaks in the woman's unnaturally black hair? Outlandish contacts, some even resembling the eyes of snakes or tigers, were only a click away for anyone with access to the internet.

Alongside a grassy field, Lisa pulled off to the shoulder. Clambering out, she sucked in mouthfuls of cool air, willing herself to drag in enough oxygen to think through the memories threatening to unhinge her, the cold voice repeating the words "Sweet Girl Baby" in her ear.

She forced herself to picture Evie with subtler blue eyes, then brown, then green, then black. But it wasn't until she thought of a woodsy green-gold hazel combined with sandy blond hair that she clapped her hands over her mouth in a vain attempt to block the scream bubbling its way up from the depths of memory.

COLE SPOTTED LISA ALONG the roadside, down on her knees with her palms pressed to her forehead. He pulled up behind her, his marrow freezing at the thought that she looked like a woman who had gotten word that the worst had happened.

Impossible, he realized, since she had no cell phone. And no business attempting to drive herself anywhere in the state she was in.

Pocketing his keys, he exited the car and walked up behind her. Though he made no effort to be quiet, she didn't even turn her head to see who was there. Didn't acknowledge him in any way.

Despite what should have been a more-than-adequate denim jacket, she was shivering violently, as if she'd been dunked into a vat of freezing water—or a nightmare neither her body nor her soul could bear any longer. When he moved to see her face, her brown eyes were unfocused, the lashes sparkling with a heavy dew of tears.

Her misery breaking down every barricade he'd built, he ached to lift her from the roadside, to haul her into his arms and warm her with his body. But more than that, raw instinct had him wanting to claim the right to protect her, to distract her with his kiss.

The wrongness of the idea jolted through him. What kind of bastard was he, to imagine she would welcome his touch? Or to think for a single moment that the fierce attraction roaring through him—and heaven forgive him, but he couldn't help the chord that her curves, her scent, her devastated beauty, had struck in his imagination— could possibly distract her from her missing son...

Her son, whose "proof of life" was proof of nothing, really, except that he'd been alive when the kidnappers took the shot yesterday.

Letting out a slow breath, he fought to gentle his voice, to still the raw fury reverberating through him at the thought of the kidnappers he wanted to rip apart with his bare hands. He had to pull himself together to have any hope of helping Lisa—and to remind himself that this was about repaying a debt to Devin Meador, not betraying a dead fellow soldier's memory by moving in on his widow.

"Hey there, you." Cole laid his hand on her shoulder. "How 'bout we get you back on your feet, and you can tell me what's happening? Or maybe we won't talk at all. We'll just go sit in the car awhile, okay?"

With almost glacial slowness, her gaze rose to meet his, the misery in her brown eyes giving way to surprise. "Cole? What are you doing here? I—"

"Thought you'd ditched me, didn't you?" he said lightly as he helped her to her feet. "On a scale of daring escapes, I'd give yours pretty high marks. If the rental clerk hadn't seemed so freaked out when I found that photo, I'd still be scratching my head."

She looked at a spot near her feet. "I'm sorry. I've put

you to so much trouble. But I had to—for Tyler. I couldn't see any other way."

Cursing himself for his inability to resist the impulse, he ran his thumb along the smooth flesh of her cheek, then tilted her chin until she was looking into his eyes. Looking, and really seeing him for the first time, judging from her expression.

"You know," he told her, smiling to lighten his words, "you've been causing me trouble ever since I met you. Must be all this excitement that keeps me coming back for more."

"Then you're a glutton for punishment, or crazy."

He smiled. "Only when it comes to war and women, sweetheart. Now why don't you take a deep breath? We need to talk, but first, if I don't let your father know you're okay, he'll have my hide next time I see him."

She nodded. "Please tell him I'm sorry."

"Tell him yourself," he suggested, taking off his jacket and draping it over her shoulders. "I know he'll be relieved to hear your voice."

She shook her head. "I can't. Not now."

"Fair enough," he said, pulling his phone from his pocket.

When Sid Hartfield answered on the first ring, Cole reported, "I've found her, safe but shaken. She wants you to know she's sorry for worrying you. I'll call you back once I know more."

True to his cop nature, the older man tried to grill him, but in the end Cole convinced him that this wasn't the time. Then he switched his phone to silent mode, so he and Lisa wouldn't be disturbed.

They'd nearly made it to his rental before she caught his arm. "No, not here. My SUV." She shook her head.

"There's something there you need to see, that's all. Something that'll make this easier to explain."

"I figured out about the card they sent," he said, as they walked to the bright red Chevy.

For just a moment she stopped, her breathing hard, the rest of her frozen solid.

He waited until she had recovered enough to climb behind the wheel beside him to continue. "You're not thinking of driving, are you?" he asked. "Not in your condition." She shook her head again, so he went on. "I haven't figured out exactly what was in the card," he said, "but I'm guessing they've demanded a meeting of some sort. You're supposed to bring a ransom, right? And absolutely no cops of any stripe, or else."

Reaching into her bag, she pulled out the card and passed it to him. "She doesn't—doesn't want my money. She wants my life for his."

He scanned the handwritten note, bile roiling in his stomach. *"Got an offer from a foreign broker, likes his little boys as sweet and cute as this one. Meet me alone before it goes down and you've got my word he'll be delivered to your sister back in Thornton safe and untouched. Unless you go to the cops."*

No wonder Lisa had freaked out and vanished without a word. A note like this was every parent's darkest nightmare.

Rather than focusing on the threat, he steered her toward the details. "Is this right? You have a sister?"

Lisa nodded. "Shelley teaches school in our hometown, Thornton, outside of Fort Worth."

So his earlier suspicions *had* been correct. "Evie" knew a whole hell of a lot about Lisa, including where she'd been raised and that she had a sister. Which meant that from the start, there'd been nothing random about the carjacking and Tyler's abduction.

The note went on to detail a time to meet—tonight at twelve thirty—but not a place, before ending with an order to check the cake box.

"Something was in the cake?" he asked.

"Under it, actually. A prepaid cell phone in a plastic bag."

"So Evie wasn't bluffing about having a local accomplice." Cole couldn't imagine the woman risking a return to Coopersville herself, but he could easily imagine her paying off some local lowlife.

"She has someone watching me. I'm sure of it," said Lisa. "Waiting to see my next move. That must be who printed out the— Wait, I know I have it in here somewhere." She dug frantically inside her purse. "There was a picture…"

"I've got it right here," Cole said, removing the photo from his shirt pocket. "You must've dropped it at the rental place before I got there. I found it in the lot."

She snatched it from him, then sighed as she touched the image of her son's face. "Thank God. If I'd lost this—"

"You haven't. And I've found you, so maybe somebody's looking out for you after all. Someone who doesn't want you walking into a trap that's sure to get you killed." Because as unlikely as it seemed, somewhere along the way, this sweet, beautiful woman had made a deadly enemy. But how? And who?

Lisa shook her head, her eyes narrowing as she warned him, "Don't think you're going to stop me; Cole. Because that woman—she *will* do this. You don't know her," she went on, tears streaming down her face. "She'll sell him to some monster just the way she said, and she'll laugh while my baby—"

"Who is she, Lisa? Because it's crystal clear that 'Evie LeStrange' knows you. And it's just as clear that you've been lying about it from the start."

CURIOUSER AND CURIOUSER, Jill thought as she watched Captain Cole Sawyer climb into the SUV with Lisa. For people who supposedly didn't know each other, they seemed to be going to great lengths to sneak around.

After seeing Lisa pull over, get out of her rental and drop to her knees sobbing, she had pulled over herself and watched from a safe distance. She understood the impulse to cry alone that must have overtaken her. Even in those first horrible days after the beating and miscarriage, she'd done everything in her power not to cry in front of anyone, because she'd long since learned that every emotional display was held as evidence that a woman wasn't up to the standard. That she wasn't strong enough to do what needed to be done.

And then Cole Sawyer had driven up, and she'd realized that, emotional breakdown aside, Lisa had come here to meet a man who might very well be a coconspirator in a robbery scheme that had backfired and ended up getting Trace hurt. And now they were taking off together, leaving Sawyer's rental behind.

Jill knew she should call this in, but the thought was followed by another rush of anger. Who the hell was Hank Stewart to advise her on how to run a marriage and kick her off a case she had every right to be part of? And the idea of handing this over to the FBI and letting them swoop in and hog the glory was even less appealing.

Forget that garbage—she had a personal stake in figuring out what these two were really up to. And since she was on her personal time now, she was free to find out— even if she had to follow them to hell itself.

"I NEVER LIED," Lisa assured Cole, her hands knotting around the wheel. "Not even by omission."

"Then what do you know now that you didn't then?" he asked. "Because I'd bet my last dollar you've figured out who she is."

"I think I might have." Unwilling to waste any more time than her full-scale meltdown had already cost her, she started the engine. "But it's not necessarily anything you'll believe. I'm not quite sure I believe it myself."

"So try me," he said. As she put the SUV in gear and pulled out, he added, "I didn't think you were going to drive."

"I lied," she admitted.

"Mind telling me exactly where we're going?"

"Yes, I do mind." She flicked him a nervous glance. "Because I know exactly what you're going to do the minute I give you the location she texted to me. You'll ruin everything by calling the authorities, or my dad, which would amount to the same thing."

As they pulled out onto the empty road, he shook his head. "Lisa, there's not a car or a house in sight. Evie can't have spies everywhere, and the FBI's much better equipped to—"

"No, Cole. This is my son, not yours, not the FBI's, and I'm not taking any chances." Her skin tightened, the fine hairs rising along her arms and behind her neck. "Especially not with a woman who can come back from the dead."

Did he think she'd lost her mind now? Would he try to overpower her? Dial 9-1-1 and get the authorities to come stop her, drawing attention with their wailing sirens and flashing lights? Once they figured out what else she'd done today, she thought guiltily, they might even throw her in jail, where she would have no say at all in how her son's case was handled.

Instead he said, "I'm listening," his voice surprisingly calm. As if he heard such crazy claims a dozen times a day.

She nodded and released the breath she had been holding. "I'll tell you the whole story, Cole, but only on one condition."

"Name it."

"When I'm finished, if you want out you can ask me to drop you someplace where you can catch a ride home, but you have to give me your word as a Ranger that you won't try to stop me."

He shook his head, avoiding her glance. "I'm not a Ranger anymore."

"I've spent enough time around the military to know one thing. *I* can leave my job, give up being a hygienist tomorrow and never look back, but you'll never really quit being a Ranger. You'll carry it inside you whether you spend the rest of your life as a U.S. Marshal or a dog-catcher."

His gaze hooked hers, his gray eyes dangerous and his strong mouth sullen. "You don't know me, Lisa Meador. You don't know what I've done, why I've moved on."

"I do know you," she said, the knowledge that she might well be driving toward her own death stripping away any need for pretense. "I know you're the kind of man who walks toward and not away from danger when it's for a good cause. The kind of man who steps up and takes responsibility where others would run screaming." *The kind of man I married once,* she thought, before realizing that Cole Sawyer, unlike the steadfast and sweet-natured Devin, still had sharp edges. He wasn't a man to be handled lightly. Or safely.

But he *was* a man to be taken at his word, if she could only wrest it from him.

"Promise," she said, "or I'll pull over and let you out right here."

"It's not that easy, Lisa. Whether I give you my word as a Ranger or a man, I don't want to risk your life. Or Tyler's. And trying to do this thing on your own—trust me, it's a bad idea."

She drove on, passing the turnoff to the Brazos River access road where they had met the fisherman in his truck. She'd blacked out there, she remembered, and yet he'd kept up the pursuit instead of abandoning the chase and turning back.

"I won't be alone," she said, her palms growing slick where she gripped the wheel. "Not if you come with me. I know you could help get Tyler and me through this."

As the miles slipped past, fat white clouds glided across a broad canvas of ice blue. Cole didn't answer for a long while but instead leaned forward, his elbows on his knees and his powerful hands laced together.

"Oh, the hell with it," he finally said.

"What's wrong?" she asked, not understanding.

Cole shook his head. "Don't worry about it. Because you have my promise, Lisa. You have my word as a man and as a Ranger that I'll do everything I can to help you. Now tell me everything you know or guess or suspect, because I've damned well earned that much."

"I GOT TO THINKING about eye color," Lisa explained. "How Evie's was so bright it looked fake, like the blue streaks in her hair. So I pictured her with different eyes, and then with different hair, too, since that's so easy to alter.

"That's when I thought of Sabra," she continued. "Sabra

Crowley, and something that happened back when I was nine."

"Sabra Crowley," he repeated, committing it to memory. "Sounds like a name for an older woman, not a child."

"I'm not sure Sabra ever was a child, not really. She and her little sister, Ava, were my dad's partner's daughters—two foster kids he and his wife eventually adopted. Ava was shy, and maybe a little odd, but she seemed like a nice girl. But from as far back as I can remember, Sabra always made me nervous. She was my sister's age, four years older, and she was seriously creepy. Worse yet, she liked to hurt things."

Lisa shuddered, hugging herself, before she could continue. "She knocked baby birds from their nests and stepped on them just to hear them crunch. Once Ava and I spied on her and saw her burying a turtle alive in a shoe box. When I dug it up and let it go later, she held me down and burned me with a cigarette lighter she'd stolen from her dad, while Ava sat there frozen, staring, so terrified that she'd be next, she couldn't say a word."

"Sounds like a budding psychopath," Cole guessed, putting it together with what he knew of Evie. "Did you tell your parents?"

"Never. I was scared to death what Sabra would do if I got her in trouble. All the neighborhood kids were. But my parents kept telling my sister and me we should be extra kind and understanding because of everything the girls had been through with their birth family. Dad never spelled out details, but I saw the looks he gave my mom, so—this will sound weird to you, considering— I felt sorry for them. Well, Ava, mostly, since she didn't have any other friends."

"That's because you're capable of empathy." Cole's

heart ached for the kind, naive girl she'd been, a child who could all too easily fall victim to the troubled older girl.

Lisa smiled sadly. "Too much of it at times, I think. Otherwise, I wouldn't have kept going over, even when Sabra tormented me, calling me Sweet Girl Baby, 'cause she'd heard my dad say it once."

She sucked in a startled breath. "She called me that. Evie, I mean, right before she made me go inside the bank. I can't believe I didn't put it together sooner. It really *was* her. Evie's Sabra, coming back somehow to hurt me in the worst way possible."

"You're sure?" he asked.

"It has to be her."

"Maybe, but why would she do this, especially so many years later?" As irrational as psychopaths could be, there must have been some trigger, but Cole couldn't imagine what Lisa could possibly have done at nine to provoke a hatred so extreme it could survive decades.

"It's because I saw Mr. Crowley—a man I called Uncle Jerry. He was back behind their shed, yelling at Sabra that he wished he'd only taken Ava and left her where she was. He was beating Sabra with his belt. I still remember the way the leather cracked against her bare legs. They were covered in welts, and some of them were bleeding."

"Son of a bitch." Cole shook his head.

"The strangest thing was, she didn't try to run or fight. She just stood there, sobbing like a baby. Her face was wet with tears and mucus. I couldn't believe it."

"What did you do?"

She shook her head. "I was so confused. The man I knew and trusted was completely out of control. I was terrified that he would spot me, that he would hurt me, too."

"He didn't see you?"

"No, but Sabra did, and she told me later that I couldn't

say anything, no matter what. That she could take anything that bald-headed bastard could dish out. Then she swore if anybody found out she was bawling, she would drag me out into the woods and—and beat my head in with a big rock and bury me where no one would ever find my body."

"Oh, Lisa. So, what happened? What did you do?"

"I couldn't tell my parents. Uncle Jerry was like part of the family. I talked to my sister, instead, and we decided together that Sabra was too dangerous to cross. And we both thought, too—I'm ashamed to admit this right now—that whatever Sabra had done to get Uncle Jerry so mad, she probably deserved that whipping. Mrs. Crowley's sweet old cat had disappeared a few weeks earlier, and we all figured Sabra had something to do with it. So I just tried to pretend I never saw it."

"You were a frightened little kid. You can't blame yourself."

"Sabra blamed me big-time after it got out. One day she got into some kind of shoving match in the hall with my sister, and I guess Shelley'd had enough of getting knocked down. She told Sabra she was a big phony who bawled like a baby when she got waled on at home. And just like that, Sabra knew I'd told. And everybody knew about her getting beaten. They laughed and tormented her about it for weeks."

"Stupid junior high kids." Cole shook his head, remembering the constant ebb and flow of cruelty. "So, did she come after you then?"

"She swore she would. She kept telling me, 'I've never backed off from a threat. Not ever. I don't care how long it takes.' I was throwing up and staying home from school, I was so terrified. And it got even worse after Mr. Crowley died."

"What happened?"

"At first everybody thought it was some awful bug he'd picked up," she said, her voice thick with emotion. "But I kept thinking about what Sabra said about getting even, how she might do anything. So finally I did what I should have from the start and told my parents everything."

Nodding, he said, "That must've taken a lot of courage."

"It was one of the hardest things I've ever done." She let out a long breath.

"So, how did your folks take it?"

"When I talked about Uncle Jerry beating Sabra, Mom gave me a big lecture about speaking ill of the dead, but my dad got really quiet. I guess there was already some question about how he really died, and Sabra's behavior had raised a lot of red flags. The next thing I heard, the police searched her room. They found rat poison hidden there. Mrs. Crowley and Ava both had to be treated for it, too."

"What a sick kid," Cole said. "So I guess she was arrested?"

"Apparently she got wind the police were looking for her. That's when she tried to run away."

"Tried to?" Cole was already thinking two steps ahead, to the part where a grown psychopath would have been released from custody—freed to exact a brand of revenge she'd had years to plan. Maybe she had somehow learned that Lisa had pointed her father and his fellow officers in her direction, or maybe she still blamed her for her humiliation at school. Whatever it was, she'd decided to pay Lisa back with interest.

Lisa nodded, releasing a shaky breath. "She hitchhiked. They think she might've been trying to get back to where her birth family came from—somewhere in west Texas.

When the police caught up with her, she—she ran into the road and— I heard later that a big truck hit her. She died instantly. They said she didn't suffer."

Cole did a double take. "Wait. You're saying that she *literally* died? This person you believe has come after you?"

"They identified her body, or what was left of it. My dad kept assuring me she was really gone, partly because I was too scared to eat, thinking she'd come back to poison me, too."

"Now you've lost me." Cole shook his head again, struggling to wrap his mind around things. "Sabra may have been one seriously warped girl, but to my knowledge, the deceased don't carry out elaborate revenge plots. The person who took Tyler had to be somebody else. Who else do you know who might have a grudge?"

But Lisa clearly wasn't ready to let go of the idea. "What if she didn't really die? What if another girl's body was mistaken for hers?"

The idea sounded seriously far-fetched, like something from an old soap opera. "Wouldn't the autopsy have revealed that? Did you ever hear of any questions about her identity?"

"No, but my parents tried not to talk about it around me if they could help it. I was already upset enough."

"What about Mrs. Crowley and Ava? Were they all right?"

"Mrs. Crowley had some sort of breakdown. She couldn't care for Ava, so she went to live with a relative or back into foster care or something like that. I never heard where."

"I hope you didn't blame yourself for what happened to that family. You were just a child. Just a scared little girl."

The clouds parted, and Lisa reached into her purse,

then pulled out dark glasses against the brilliant Texas sun. Slipping them on, she said, "Of course I blamed myself. For a very long time. I kept thinking that if I'd only told my dad what I'd seen sooner, Sabra wouldn't have killed Uncle Jerry. She wouldn't have died, either, and Mrs. Crowley and Ava would both still be safe at home."

"You can't let yourself go back there," Cole said, thinking how much easier it was to give that advice than take it.

After the incident in the marketplace, his fellow Rangers and his superiors had all noticed the change in his behavior. Under orders from the government to curb the alarming trend of soldier suicides, his C.O. had forced him to see an army shrink, who had quickly decided that Cole wasn't the type to take the easy exit of a noose or bullet.

But the dangers didn't end there, the shrink had told him. The guilt he felt—completely unwarranted, the psychiatrist had insisted—might easily manifest itself in other self-destructive behaviors, such as dangerous risk-taking.

Cole knew the man had been thinking in terms of substance abuse or adrenaline-soaked sports. He would be willing to bet the doctor would be surprised as hell to learn that the greatest risk would be the promise of redemption in the form of a beautiful widow with a problem he couldn't turn away from, a woman he somehow needed as badly as she needed him.

But despite all that counseling, how many times had he gone back to his first glimpse of the woman in the snow-white burka? How often had he imagined pulling the trigger before she reached the detonator switch? For all of his regrets and every tortured fantasy, those people were still just as dead as his taste for his job.

Including, God forgive him, Lisa's husband.

"There's no way you can know what might have happened if you'd acted earlier, and there's nothing you can do about it now," he continued, parroting the army shrink's useless words. "And there's absolutely no use tormenting yourself for—"

"For getting Tyler kidnapped and, at best, emotionally scarred for life? How am I supposed to live with that, Cole? You tell me, and I'll do it."

"I don't know the answer to that, Lisa. But I do know that I mean to do my damnedest to get him home safely—and get you out of this alive."

She shifted uncomfortably in her seat before admitting, "I made a stop before I left town."

"Where?"

"After I picked up some cash from an ATM, I dropped by a friend's house because I knew she and her husband would both be working."

"What did you do, Lisa?" he asked, already guessing he wasn't going to like the answer.

"I used a rock to break a window, and I climbed inside. I took—"

"Are you crazy?" he asked, alarm streaking through him. "That's a felony."

Frowning at the interruption, she continued. "I took a pistol I knew she keeps in a nightstand next to her bed. I took it to kill Sabra, and I will, if that's what it takes to get Tyler back."

"You really thought you could waltz into a place of Evie's choosing and take her out?" Convinced as Lisa seemed, he still wasn't ready by a long shot to concede that Lisa was right about this Sabra returning from the dead.

"I hoped I'd get the chance, and who knows? Maybe

I still will. Sabra remembers me as the naive little girl she liked to torture, the girl too afraid to tell when she burned me with that lighter and twisted my flesh until I was covered in bruises."

He grimaced. "No one noticed the marks?"

Lisa shrugged. "I got very good at hiding things, just like Sabra hid her legs and Ava hid whatever her sister did to her. But I'm not that child anymore, Cole. I'm a woman and a mother, a mother willing to do anything, to face anyone, for the chance to raise my son."

"Whoever this Evie really is," he said, "she's crazy and she's ruthless. Against a person like that, you don't stand a chance. That's why you need to call the authorities and let them set up a perimeter, get snipers into place and a team to track her and her partner's movements."

"No." The look Lisa shot his way was half hostility, half terror. "I told you, I'm going to do this my way. You gave me your word."

"I agreed not to call and report what you're up to," he told her. "But I never promised not to try to convince you to let me do it."

Her hands tightened on the wheel, and her body stiffened. That lush, sweet body that was going to end up in the ground unless he either talked her out of this or figured out how to protect her.

"Listen, Lisa," he said gently. "You're exhausted, in shock, worried sick about your son. You're not yourself at all—hell, you've climbed out a second-story window and broken into your friend's house—"

"I left her a note apologizing." The justification sounded weak, and she looked as if she knew it. "I told her I'd pay for any damages."

"A written confession. Even better." Cole shook his

head. "Seriously, how can you possibly trust yourself to be making good decisions right now?"

"The real question," she said, turning to glare at him, "is how can I possibly trust anyone else with my son's life?"

Chapter Thirteen

Cole skewered her with a look. "What about your father? How would *you* feel if *he* sneaked off without a word of explanation?"

Guilt swamped her. He was right. "Can you text him for me? Let him know I'm with you and I'm all right, but we may be out of touch for a while?"

"Lisa, he's going crazy. I already have a half dozen missed calls from him."

"Send the text," she repeated, then realized that it wouldn't satisfy her father. Frantic as he must be, he might have called the authorities already.

"As soon as you're finished," she told Cole, "I'll need the battery from your phone. Otherwise, someone could use the GPS to find us."

"If the dental hygienist thing doesn't work out for you," he said irritably, "maybe you should check out a life of crime. You're starting to show a real knack for it."

"So I like mystery novels, and my father was a cop," she said. "But let's get one thing straight, Cole. That doesn't make me a criminal any more than standing in a garage makes me a car."

He smiled at that and added, "Or attempting to rob a bank makes you a—"

She pulled over abruptly, wheels screeching, the tires

sending up a plume of dust. "You can walk from here. Or hitch a ride. If you think for one minute that I was in on some kind of conspiracy that got my son kidnapped..."

"I was joking, Lisa," he said, his words slow and decisive. "Seriously, how many master criminals do you figure leave signed apology notes? Now, if you're finished being touchy, I'll go ahead and text your father."

She looked away, embarrassed by her outburst. She was acting like Tyler when he was sick or tired. Lashing out at the very person who only meant to help her.

Cole worked on his text, taking forever to word the message exactly as he wanted. Once he'd handed over the phone and battery, he remained locked in stony silence for mile upon mile. Lisa had no idea whether he was regretting his decision or trying to dream up other tactics to change her mind, but with her body aching with exhaustion and her brain swirling with anxiety, she was in no mood to try to pry a conversation from a rock.

She took the turnoff that would put them on I-10 West, her conscience stinging as she passed the sign for the Texas Two-Step in Coffee Creek. As soon as this was over, she needed to thank the owner for her generosity and repay the woman for the phone she'd lost.

As soon as this was over... Would it ever be? Would she ever again see Tyler playing with his plastic dinosaurs in front of cartoons, sneaking his last, detested bite of broccoli to Rowdy, wrapping his little arms around her neck and giggling at the loud smacking noises she made as she kissed him?

Her head began to throb again, and her stomach started churning. Grumbling with hunger, she realized, and felt the same punch of guilt that accompanied each emergence of her body's needs. But a glance at the dashboard clock informed her that they'd been on the road for hours, and she couldn't remember when she'd last eaten anything of substance.

About twenty minutes after they merged onto the interstate, she spotted a sign for a fuel and convenience store. But what if Cole had changed his mind? What if he used the stop as a chance to leave her?

Shaking off the worry—she couldn't very well expect to make it to Terlingua, Texas, without stopping—she told him, "Seems like a good place for a pit stop. Anything you want?"

He speared her with a look of irritation. "Your trust would be a great start. Seems like I've earned it by now."

"I was thinking more in terms of the sandwich counter," she said, reminding herself to think of food as only another form of fuel.

"Which means, I take it, that we'll be on the road for some time?"

"We'll be on I-10 West for hours," she said carefully, "so I'd advise you to take advantage of the stop."

"All right. Let me top off your gas tank while we're here, too," he said, pulling a credit card from his wallet.

"I'll be paying cash inside," she said, since she had no intention of allowing anyone to track her movements via credit card use.

Cole shot her an annoyed look, then passed her a twenty as they pulled up to a pump. "Ham and cheese with the works is good for me. Maybe some chips and an iced tea, too. I'll be inside in a minute."

She tried to give him back his money, but he turned away to deal with the gas.

She should have been ready to leave before him, but thanks to a line for the ladies' room, followed by a seriously undermotivated sandwich maker at the counter, he was back in the SUV ahead of her—sitting behind the wheel.

Juggling the drinks and sandwiches to open the door on his side, she frowned at him. "Thanks for the thought, but I need you to move over."

His gray eyes skewered her, a gaze so clear and penetrating that she felt the world drop away beneath her as she imagined what it might be like to have that laserlike intensity focused on her in a far more intimate setting. To feel him naked with his arms around her, his blazing kisses banishing all memory of this past week.

Horrified, she looked away, face flaming at another of her body's traitorous demands. What kind of woman was she to think of Cole that way, even for a moment, with Tyler's life hanging in the balance and the husband she had dearly loved dead barely a year?

A tired, freaked-out woman, she tried to tell herself, struggling to chalk her feelings up to stress and put it out of her mind. Yet the thought of that taut, hard-muscled body naked was a bell that couldn't be unrung. One she couldn't forgive herself for any more than she could bear to look into his handsome face.

"You're going to let me drive now," he said gruffly, "and you're going to sleep awhile before you fall asleep at the wheel."

Still upset at herself, she dredged up a little righteous indignation. Who was this man—a man who'd referred to himself as a washed-up army Ranger, for heaven's sake— to order her around? "So, how's that going to work," she snapped, "if I'm the only one who knows where we're heading?"

"You said yourself, we'll be on I-10 West for hours. Just tell me when to wake you up."

She thought about what he could do if she gave in to her

exhaustion. He could call the authorities, her father—the cavalry, for that matter—and she would probably sleep right through it.

Yet as she calmed down, she thought of other things, as well. How much he'd already done for her, risked for her. And in exchange for all that, he had asked for only one thing. *Your trust would be a great start.*

"I've watched you nearly nod off two or three times in the last hour," he said. "If you think I'm letting you get behind the wheel again to get us killed, or maybe hurt or kill another driver, I'll stay here and catch a ride home. Is that what you want, Lisa? To do this on your own?"

"I'll trust you, Cole," she told him, because he was right. What choice did she really have? None, not with her body turning on her, and her sleep-deprived brain fantasizing about his mouth feasting on her neck, his hands moving up beneath her shirt to...

More disturbed than ever, she shook off the images and reminded herself that she would need all her faculties to be ready for Sabra tonight at twelve thirty. All her faculties, and every bit of luck that she could muster.

IT WASN'T AS EASY as people thought to tail someone without being noticed. Jill was forced to hang far back, often allowing several cars to get between her and her quarry. Several times she lost the red SUV, including once when she'd been forced to make a quick stop off the interstate to use a restroom and get gas.

She was distracted again later when Trace's sister Ella called her.

"I thought you'd want to know," she said. "He's come out of his coma."

The news tore a whoop of pure joy from Jill, followed

by a question. "How's his—the head injury. Is he…?" *Is he still Trace?*

"He's a little groggy, but he's making sense and speaking pretty clearly. Asking for you, mostly."

"For me?" Warmth flooded her veins and arteries, suffused every cell with pure emotion. It took her a moment to realize it was hope.

"Of course," Ella explained, "Mom reminded him the two of you are divorced. To tell you the truth, I think she's a little miffed that he woke up more concerned about your condition than his own."

"You told him I'm fine, right? That I got away with only bumps and bruises?" And a raging case of guilt for leading her normally straitlaced ex-husband to ignore Sheriff Stewart's orders and nearly getting both of them killed.

"Mom was only too happy to tell him that you got off scot-free." Ella had the grace to sound embarrassed. "Sorry."

Jill tightened her death grip on the wheel. "I don't care about that right now. What about his legs? Can he…?"

"He's still numb. But he did wiggle two left toes a little. Or at least that's what my mom swears."

"Doesn't that mean he might get better?"

"You can tell the doctors are being careful not to get our hopes up too high," Ella explained, "but they say that once the swelling goes down, there's a good chance he'll recover some more movement—and that it's very possible the spinal cord is only compressed and not severed."

"I want to come see him," Jill blurted.

"I don't think that's a good idea. Not now."

"But he's *asking* for me."

"He was," Ella said softly, before hurriedly adding, "I'd

better go. Mom's coming." Without saying goodbye, she broke the connection.

It was only then that Jill realized the SUV she'd been trailing was nowhere in sight. A bubble of panic pressed against her pounding heart. Maybe this was a sign, the universe's way of saying that she should turn around and drive straight to Austin, whether Trace's family wanted her there or not.

But what if Trace didn't, either? If he realized she truly was the root of all his troubles? How would she survive if he rejected her again?

COLE HAD LONG SINCE finished his meal before Lisa made it even halfway through her late lunch, until finally she gave up and bagged it with the trash. He watched as she drew up her knees, then twisted her arms first one way and then another in an attempt to find a comfortable position. But each time she seemed to doze for a few moments, she would twitch violently and jerk awake, crying Tyler's name.

Cole's chest ached to witness her torment, and inside him, the pressure mounted to somehow fix this for her. To chuck everything he hoped to be and set out to find the man he'd been. The man who would bring home both Lisa and her innocent child or die trying.

It was too damned bad he'd left the best part of that man back among the carnage of that crowded marketplace in Lashkar Gah. What if he failed Lisa and her child just as miserably as he had failed her husband and the innocent civilians who'd died that day?

As Lisa whimpered in her sleep, he told himself that this was about something a lot more important than his own fears. That this was one challenge too big to back away from.

"It's going to be all right, I promise." He reached out, his fingers stroking the soft skin on the back of her hand. But it wasn't enough, not nearly, so he gave in to the impulse to twine his fingers through hers.

The beautiful brown eyes fluttered, and for a moment she peered at him through half-lowered lids. But instead of pulling away with a warning not to touch her, she closed her eyes once more, a soft sigh slipping free.

"You're safe with me," he murmured. "Safe to rest now."

He kept hold for a long while, until her breathing lengthened and her grip relaxed. Once he was certain she was truly sleeping, he carefully disentangled his hand from hers and prayed she'd found her way to a place untroubled by dark dreams or her even darker waking nightmare.

As the interstate sliced its way through west Texas, the land opened up into rolling rangeland cracked with craggy ravines and dotted with thorny clumps of mesquite. Good hunting land, judging from the number of deer blinds he spotted, tiny house-shaped shells elevated on stilts just above the ground.

But the quarry he was contemplating had no open season, and unlike the deer, Evie and her partner would be armed, a mismatch made even more lopsided since he had turned in his handgun to the sheriff's office to aid in the joint task force investigation.

Time to do something about that, he thought, reaching over and snagging the handle of Lisa's purse. Dropping it into his lap, he felt around inside it, then came up with the gun that she had "borrowed" from her friend's house.

"Sorry," he whispered to the sleeping woman. "But I'm way more likely to put this to good use than you are."

After tucking it out of her reach in the map pocket, he

took out an unfamiliar cell phone. Knowing it must be the same one she had mentioned finding under the cake, he pulled onto the shoulder for a closer look.

After glancing over to be sure she hadn't awakened, he found nothing in either the phone's address book or call log, nothing at all beyond one text message that had come from a blocked number. It contained only a pair of numbers that looked suspiciously like latitude and longitude coordinates.

Clearly Lisa had surmised the same thing. She must have looked up the location using the laptop he'd spotted in her bedroom earlier. But a smartphone would work just as well, so after a guilty glance at Lisa, he pulled out his phone and replaced the battery she had taken. Bristling with impatience, he waited for the phone to acquire a signal. Fortunately it was a good one, thanks to the cell towers along the interstate.

The first thing that popped up were alerts showing numerous missed calls, voice mails and text messages from Lisa's dad. Ignoring them, he went to the GPS app and typed in the numbers Evie had given Lisa.

Within seconds, he discovered their destination: an old cemetery in the mostly abandoned mining town of Terlingua, Texas. Another click revealed that the former ghost town currently had a couple hundred or so residents, many of whom apparently eked out their livings working in local tourist traps. But at 12:30 a.m., the only people he expected to encounter at their dark and lonely meeting place were the kidnappers, including the monster who clearly meant to leave Lisa lying there among the dead.

One glance at the woman sleeping in the seat beside him convinced him that she would never back down from her plan to save her child, even if it meant sacrificing her own life. Though he still believed her decision to act without the authorities on her side was far too risky, she was correct about one thing. This was a call no one else had the right to make for her, because either way there would be dangers, so the consequences would be hers to live with.

At least they would be if she lived. That was where he came in, seeing that she survived to bring Tyler home, whether or not the boy survived.

Though Cole would have loved to believe Evie's promise to send Tyler, safe and sound, to Lisa's sister, he didn't buy it for a second. Whoever the woman was, she'd proven herself to be the kind of psychopath who would never pass up a cash buyer, no matter what she'd claimed.

And if he meant to stop her, he couldn't go in blind, nor could he ignore the one possible lead Lisa had come up with. With time running short, he couldn't afford to wait around on the side of the road.

Before he left, however, he checked his text messages to see if Lisa's father had responded to the questions he'd asked about Sabra Crowley when he'd first messaged to let the man know Lisa was all right.

"Why ask me about old business?" Hartfield had responded. *"What the hell is going on now?"*

Cole grimaced, seeing that the older man's earlier texts consisted of demands, each more impatient than the last, that Cole immediately call him. Furious as Hartfield was, Cole conceded there was no way to get the information that he needed without risking a conversation.

He glanced over at Lisa once more, making sure she was still sleeping. Praying she would stay that way, he climbed out of the SUV, then left the door barely open behind him as he stepped around the back of the vehicle to make the call.

He didn't even hear the phone ring before Hartfield was on the line and snarling, "Where the hell are you two? I've been pacing holes in the rugs waiting for you two to get back home."

"I'm sorry, sir. I made a promise to your daughter that I wouldn't share any intel on where we are or where we're heading."

"Well, break it."

"Sorry. I can't do that."

"You *won't,* you mean, right?"

"I don't give my word lightly. And I don't break it at all."

"She's had a message, hasn't she?" her father guessed. "Those kidnappers contacted her somehow."

Cole let his silence answer for him.

"Don't be an idiot, Sawyer. She'll get herself or my grandson—maybe both of them—killed if she goes to meet those people!" There was no disguising the fear that lurked behind Hartfield's anger. "Ransom exchanges never work out."

"That's why I thought it would be better if she had me with her. Otherwise, she would have gone by herself. And you need to know, they're not demanding ransom."

"Then what?"

Cole weighed how much to say. "They're guaranteeing the boy's safety in exchange for a meeting. No law enforcement, no one else. Just your daughter, alone."

"Then all this, it's about setting Lisa up for— If anything happens to my girl, I can guarantee you, I'm going to see so much hellfire rained down on top of your head, you'll be beggin' to go back to the war zone."

"That's certainly your prerogative, sir. But know this. Other than breaking faith with your daughter, I'll do whatever I have to, to see that she and your grandson both come home safely. I give you my word on that."

"You better pray that that's enough, boy."

"Believe me, I will," Cole said honestly. "Now, before Lisa wakes up and gives me holy hell for making this call, tell me everything you know about Sabra Crowley."

"She's dead. What else do you need to know?"

"I don't have time to make you understand. Just tell me everything."

Hartfield gave a long sigh. "That was one disturbed kid, and one hell of a bad family situation. I thought my partner did a fine thing taking her and Ava home while they still stood some chance. If you'd have seen 'em, half-starved and black-and-blue, you'd have understood. Even though it all went to hell, you'd have known that Jerry meant to do the right thing."

"So you knew he was beating her? You knew and you did nothing?" Cole demanded.

"Hell no. I didn't know a thing till Lisa told me after Jerry died, or I swear I would've stopped him, would've gotten him help or even locked up my best friend if I had to."

"What about Sabra's body? Did you ever see it?"

"Much as I wanted her punished for what she did to Jerry, it was bad." Cole heard the ghost of sadness in Hartfield's voice. "Real bad. The girl was hit by a truck doing about sixty. The mother was too upset to see her, so I was asked to do the ID. And I swear it was Sabra. Her hair, her clothes, and the backpack she had on her had her belongings in it."

"So it was just the backpack? They didn't use dental records for the ID, or fingerprints or—"

"Enough with all these questions!" Hartfield exploded. "You want to know any more, you'll tell me what my partner's murder and this girl's death could possibly have to do with my grandson's abduction."

"Lisa thinks the woman who carjacked her is Sabra.

But if Sabra really was killed—" Suddenly he heard Lisa, sounding frantic as she called his name. "I have to go," he told her father.

"Wait a minute, boy," Sid Hartfield said urgently. "I need to tell you—"

But it was too late. Cole was already switching off the phone—and facing Lisa's wrath.

"WHAT ARE YOU doing?" she demanded. Was he *trying* to get them traced, using his phone in an attempt to get around his promise? "Give me that. I told you—"

"It's fine," he said, popping out the battery and handing it over. "They can't trace things that fast."

"I trusted you to keep driving," she said, fear clenching inside her as cars rushed past on the freeway. "How long have we been parked here?"

"Five minutes, tops," he told her. "As worried as your dad was, I knew if I didn't touch base, he'd have the FBI or the sheriff on us for sure, and they'd catch us before we ever made it to Terlingua."

"How do you know…?" Her stomach lurched as she realized what he had done. "You checked out the other phone, didn't you? And saw Evie's text." It wasn't a question.

"You bet I did. Did you really expect me to walk into the situation without all the information?"

Her eyes narrowed. "You took my gun, too, didn't you?"

"You think I wanted to end up looking down a barrel if you caught me using the phone?" he asked as headed back toward the driver's seat.

"Give it back, Cole," she said, walking up behind him. "Give it back to me now."

He turned and slanted her a look. "If I didn't think

you'd be safe with it before, what makes you think I'd suddenly hand it back *after* pissing you off?"

He sounded so darned cocky, she popped his shoulder with her palm in frustration. She might as well have smacked a brick wall for all the good it did her. Turning away, she walked around the vehicle and climbed back inside.

Cole buckled his seat belt and started up the SUV.

"So, that's it, isn't it?" she asked, tears burning. "You've taken away my gun, and now you're taking me back home, too, aren't you? You and my dad have decided you know best, and you're going to force me…"

She couldn't squeeze another word past the dread building at the thought of how highly visible an official operation would be in a tiny little ghost town. Whether it was instinct or intuition, she knew in her heart that she needed to do this on her own. To do whatever she had to do to appease Sabra rather than escalate the situation.

A phone chimed—the disposable cell that Sabra had sent. Breath ripping from her lungs, Lisa fumbled to answer, only to discover that it wasn't a call coming but some kind of message. "How am I supposed to answer this?" she asked Cole.

He leaned over to see the screen. "Click the icon. Right there."

Trembling, she did, her marrow freezing as the digital video began to play. Poorly lit and out of focus, it was a close-up of her son's face. His hair was mussed, and he looked tired as he stared into the camera.

"Hurry, Mommy. Hurry, please. She says you gotta come all by yourself, or something bad will—"

The message stopped abruptly.

"Why?" she sobbed. "Why do this to Tyler? *I'm* the

one who didn't help her when I should have. *I'm* the one who should be punished."

Leaning over the console, Cole pulled her into an embrace. An embrace that felt, just for a moment, like the only thing preventing her from flying to pieces.

"Don't try to make sense of it," he whispered as he rocked her gently, his fingers stroking her hair. "It's simply cruelty, Lisa, an attempt to scare you into playing into her hands."

Pushing herself free, she said, "You heard what she said. I have to go alone."

"She can't possibly know I'm coming with you," Cole said. "She's like any other terrorist, using intimidation to keep you off balance."

He sounded so reasonable, so calm and rational, that she struggled to fight her way clear of hysteria. "Coming with me. Then you're not taking me home?"

"I was never planning on taking you home, Lisa."

"Really?"

"I gave you my word, didn't I? I'm just trying to find some way to do it so that promise won't end up costing you your life. Now buckle up so we can get back on the road. We need to get going if you want to make Terlingua in time."

Relief flowed over her, a warm, tingling sensation cascading through her nervous system. She'd been right about his inability to break his vow, right about the man that he was, for all his headstrong gruffness. Buckling up, she thanked God that her instincts had been right.

As he merged with traffic, she thought about what he had just said.

"You mean to try to ambush the ambushers, don't you?" she asked, speaking in hushed tones.

"Well, I'd rather have something better to do it with

than this girlie little .22," he said with a maddeningly off-hand shrug, "but, yeah, that's the general plan. And given the right shot, this gun's quite capable of killing someone. Those smaller rounds just love to bounce around inside a person's brainpan and wreak havoc."

She closed her eyes for a moment, painfully reminded that her husband had died after a piece of shrapnel from the bombing did the same thing.

"I won't kill them unless I have to," he said. "Especially not if they don't have Tyler with them. But I don't want to kid you. It'll be tough, maybe impossible, to take down a well-armed opponent without a kill shot. The best we can hope for is the element of surprise."

At the mention of her son's name, she'd been gripped with the desire to replay the video, to see his face again, even if it was for no more than a few wrenching moments. As if he sensed her struggle, Cole drew her into a conversation about their exit off the interstate and the route they would take south, into the remote Big Bend. She pulled a Texas road map she'd brought from the glove box and studied roads that would take them through deserts and among mountains before they reached Terlingua hours after dark.

But the longer they discussed it, the more apprehension tightened her stomach. No matter when they arrived or how stealthily Cole moved into whatever position he judged would be most advantageous, it was all too easy to imagine someone spotting him. Or Sabra mowing them down before Lisa ever got the chance to beg forgiveness for the sin that had set this nightmare into motion.

Chapter Fourteen

Jill had finally spotted the red Chevy, and as she drove, she allowed the hum of her tires on the highway to convince her that it wasn't fear of rejection keeping her from turning around, it was the pursuit of justice.

She realized now that she should have called this in hours ago, when she'd first spotted the couple heading out of town together, then bulled her way into Trace's room in Austin before his family reminded him that she was now the enemy.

But she'd screwed up, doing neither, and like a dog that had snatched its owner's thawing T-bone from the counter, she was too committed to her transgression to give up her prize now.

Several hours later she was doing about seventy when the car began to pull to the right. Listening carefully, she groaned, her stomach sinking with the realization that, of all the damned luck, she had a flat, out here on this dark road, miles and miles from help.

Pulling over, she got out and confirmed that the right front tire was going down fast. She popped the trunk to pull out the spare, sighing as her quarry, already far ahead of her, disappeared once more.

But she had changed flats before. Dirty and greasy as the job was, there was nothing to it, really.

She would rather do it ten times over than admit she'd been wrong in following the couple.

In spite of Lisa's protests, Cole insisted that they stop for a meal in Alpine before the last leg of their journey, the nearly two-hour drive to Terlingua. They needed to stretch their legs, to regroup and refocus their concentration before he could present his plan—and make certain she understood exactly how risky this face-to-face would be.

But mostly he had to be sure that she understood everything, including exactly who had agreed to help her. Because she deserved the truth of his involvement in her husband's death before she decided to put both her life and Tyler's into his hands.

Still, it was a tale he dreaded telling, almost as much as he hated explaining why he hadn't come clean from the start. But he owed her too much to turn coward, even if she would hate him for what he had to say.

Hours after the lavish west Texas sunset had painted the sky crimson, it had gone an inky black, studded with the myriad stars the area was known for. But as they entered the steak house recommended by the clerk at the convenience store where they bought fuel, he could see in Lisa's eyes that she wasn't thinking about the beauty of the desert sky, only the frightened little boy who was facing another night without her.

If I have anything to say about it, he swore, *he'll be in your arms by morning.*

As their waitress, a blowsy, middle-aged blonde who wore cowboy boots with her denim skirt, filled their water glasses, she asked, "You hear the big news?"

When Lisa tensed, the blonde spilled it, sounding almost gleeful. "That missing tourist over at Big Bend

Park—they found her body in the Chisos Mountain Basin, along a closed trail where she was hiking on her own."

"Climbing accident?" Cole asked, eager to get rid of her so he and Lisa could talk.

"Nope. They're sayin' it was a mountain lion. First lion attack around these parts in years."

To Cole's surprise, Lisa had a question. "Is that anywhere near Terlingua?"

"Maybe thirty miles as the crow flies. Why's that?"

She shrugged in answer before asking, "Will they kill it?"

"Park rangers're hunting it with dogs, I hear, but I hope that lion's halfway to Mexico by now," the waitress told her fiercely. "Cougar's got a right to eat, same as you and me, and if some tourist's dumb enough to hike those trails alone at dusk, well, I say that's just nature, pickin' off the weak."

The woman went on to recommend the rib eye, adding with a wink, "I'll tell you, there's nothing like rare Texas meat."

Looking horrified, Lisa ordered a vegetable plate, while Cole, who never turned down a good steak if he could help it, went with the waitress's suggestion.

As it turned out, neither of them had much appetite for the food. Especially not once Cole started going over the details of a mission that could so easily go fatally wrong.

Putting down his fork with more than half his meal uneaten, he reached across the table to touch the back of her hand. "There's still time to change your mind, Lisa. Time to call in help if—"

She took his hand and squeezed it, her beautiful brown eyes locked with his. "I *have* help, Cole. I have *you*."

The faith in her expression—the gratitude, of all things—sent fresh guilt crashing through him. He'd been lying by omission, allowing her to think he was some sort of damned hero. Allowing himself to think about her not only as Devin Meador's desperate widow, but as a woman. A woman he hated himself for caring about, for—hell, why not admit it?—*wanting* more with every passing hour.

"Back at your house this morning," he managed, a band of pressure tightening around his skull, "you asked why I would come back. Why I'd want to do this."

She shook her head. "I don't care why, Cole. I only thank God that you did."

"Don't thank God," he said. "Thank your husband."

Eyes widening, she pulled her hand into her lap. "What? Did you know Devin? Why didn't you say—"

"I didn't know him," he admitted, "but I—I was there, Lisa. Thirteen months ago, in Lashkar Gah."

She stared at his face, studying him as if she'd never seen him before. "What are you saying?"

"I'm saying I was part of the team that responded to a report of a woman who might be rigged with explosives."

Her face went white as paper. "You mean you…you tried to stop her."

"We encountered trouble on the way in," he said. "An ambush, like the whole thing might've been some kind of setup. But I should've stopped her anyway. Should've got my shot off in time."

She skewered him with a stricken look. "*Could* you have saved him?"

He closed his eyes, reliving that split-second hesitation and the fiery concussion that had followed. Remembering the physical and mental agony. "Yes. I could have saved him. Could have saved them all. And I will carry that knowledge—and that guilt—with me forever."

He forced himself to look at her, to face the judgment in her eyes. "I'm sorry, Lisa. Sorry I didn't tell you earlier, after I'd found out everything I could about Devin and your family." He shook his head, regret roaring through him. "Sorry I didn't defy orders by going to see you months ago, the way I wanted, to explain what really happened. But most of all, I regret that I let everyone down that day in that marketplace."

She sat there for several minutes, her eyes misted with emotion. When she finally spoke, her voice was soft and shaky. "It's why you left the army, isn't it? It's what you meant when you said you were a failed Ranger."

"It is," he admitted. "Lisa, I just wanted you to know, I'm no hero. I'm only a man, a man who'll do my very best to get you and Tyler safely home."

Her gaze snapped to his and held it, her eyes blazing, despite the moisture gleaming in them. "This time, your *very best* had better be enough, Cole Sawyer, because I can't lose my son, too. I won't. Do you understand me?"

"You won't lose him," he said, a promise that he had no business making. "I swear it on my honor. I swear it on my life."

"You'd better be right," she said. "Because if you fail Tyler the way you failed my husband, I swear I'll kill you myself."

Nodding stiffly, he signaled for the waitress, who hustled over with an offer of to-go boxes and a check that he insisted on paying. Once they left the restaurant, they both lapsed into silence, both of them wrung out from the conversation, along with the knowledge of what they were heading into.

"Just for the sake of argument," he said, changing the subject to the practical, "who else might hold a grudge against you? Who might want to hurt you by taking Tyler?"

She speared him with a hard look before releasing a

breath and shaking her head. "I've been over it and over it with the investigators, and with my father, too. But there's absolutely no one else I can come up with but Sabra. No one I can think of who'd have any reason—"

"Remember, whoever this woman is, she *isn't* reasonable, so whatever you come up with may not seem like anything. It could be someone you once beat out for a job or a previous girlfriend of your husband's. Or maybe it goes as far back as a girl who accused you of flirting with her crush in junior high, or stealing her spot on the cheerleading squad."

"Honestly, there's nothing like that I can think of, not a single enemy. Well, not unless you count the woman who schedules patients at work, but Beatrice is just mad at life in general, not me in particular."

"You're certain, Lisa? Think hard."

"I have, and I swear to you. I can't think of anyone who's this cruel and warped but Sabra."

"But Evie can't be Sabra," Cole insisted. "Not when she was killed by that truck. Your father said it looked like her. And it was her backpack."

"You asked my dad about her?" she asked accusingly.

"I make no apologies for that. I needed to know everything. Including information that might have been kept from a child at the time."

She nodded, realizing he could be right. "Was there anything I didn't tell you? Any possibility that backpack could have been stolen, or passed off to another girl?"

"Your dad's convinced it was really Sabra."

"So they weren't just telling me that so I'd stop having nightmares?"

"I don't think so."

Shaking her head, she insisted, "I think she set it up.

Gave her things to a girl she met on the run. A girl who looked like her."

Cole had heard of cases where medical examiners had gotten complacent, identifying the body they'd expected to find rather than the one actually lying on the table. Still, he couldn't believe that Sabra could have found a double, supplied her with her clothes and backpack and then… what, exactly? Shoved her into traffic?

"It's way too complicated," he said. "I can't picture her getting away with it."

"That's because you've never met her. When it came to hurting others, she was incredibly devious."

"Incredibly deranged, from the sound of it."

Lisa lowered her face to her hands. "If I'd only told my dad what I saw sooner. Now Sabra means to see I get exactly what she thinks I've got coming. I know it. But I'd rather face her a thousand times over than let her hurt my son."

"And I'd rather square off against a tank than let her, or whoever this Evie really is, hurt *you*," he vowed.

"YOU'RE SURE she said Terlingua?" From what little Deputy Jill Keller had seen—and mostly heard—of the bosomy blonde waitress, it would appear that the woman was a hell of a lot better at talking than listening to what anybody had to say.

But questioning the clerk at the first gas stop she came to had led Jill this far, and she was fresh out of other leads.

"Yep, it was Terlingua, all right," said the waitress. "I was fixin' to ask 'em if they were headin' out tonight in the dark—I can't imagine what for. I mean, it's a danged ghost town, not Las Vegas. But I didn't ask, 'cause she started actin' kind of funny right then, just because I said that mountain lions can't be faulted for pickin' off the occasional nitwit tourist."

"What's the quickest route?" Jill asked. "I need to catch up with them fast."

"You really thinking of leaving this time of night?" The waitress shook her head. "I'm tellin' you, you won't be able to see your hand in front of your face out there, much less—"

Jill pointed out her badge and snapped, "I'm sure you understand why I can't give you any details."

Minutes later, she was speeding out of Alpine and away from her own life, with all its complications. But no matter how hard she pressed down on the pedal, Jill could not outrun the memory of Trace's joy on the night she'd accepted his proposal, or his laughter as he'd spun her in his arms after she had told him they were expecting their first child.

As she hurtled through the star-strewn darkness, she wiped away hot tears, realizing for the first time what her anger, pride and no-holds-barred approach to her career had cost her....

But utterly unable to imagine a way back.

She headed past a tower visible only because of its red lights, a last, lonely vestige before the black expanse of desert. A cell tower, she dimly registered, as her long-silent phone began to ring.

As the scattered lights of Terlingua came into view, Cole pulled off the otherwise-deserted road and killed the headlights. "This is where I get out, Lisa. You won't see me when you get there, but you can bet I'll be watching you."

He remembered looking down a gun barrel, watching another young woman in another desert town. Watching and hesitating, until it was too late. He would be damned if he would make that same mistake this time.

Unable to say more, he left the SUV and started walking, the growing lump in his throat a mute testament to the turmoil inside him. But as he'd learned long ago, some things were best left bottled. Now was the time to prepare for action, not sit around and fret over what could go wrong, or imagine how things might have gone had Lisa been anyone but Devin Meador's widow. So what if she'd touched something inside him, something that he'd thought he would never feel again?

He heard her footsteps coming fast behind him, crunching on the gravel.

"Wait," said Lisa, catching at the sleeve of his jacket. But it was the emotion in her voice that stopped him, a raw echo of the turmoil he'd been struggling to lock inside.

"Please, Cole," she added. "I have to tell you how much—how much this means to me. I'm sorry for what I said before. No matter what happened in Afghanistan, you didn't have to help me. You could have walked away a hundred times."

"I tried to tell myself the same thing, but there's no way I could have—"

"A lot of men would have. We both know that. So whatever happened thirteen months ago, whatever happens tonight, I want you to know that I think you're one of the bravest men I've ever—"

He turned and pulled her to him, silencing her with a hard and angry kiss. Because he couldn't bear to let her finish, to allow her to believe that he was worthy of comparison to a man like her husband, who had made the ultimate sacrifice to serve his country, while he himself hadn't even had the strength of purpose to shoot a single suicide bomber without a fatal hesitation.

Instead of getting angry and pulling away to slap him, as he half expected, Lisa kissed him back, pouring every bit of sweetness she had to offer into their connection. It was like fire meeting water, the steam rising to engulf him. Because what he felt from her wasn't simply gratitude, but a shocking urgency, a passionate need that started a moan low in her throat. A sound that swept aside his anger and had his hands racing along forbidden curves.

Too fast, and far too greedily, but instead of jerking away, she pressed closer as she slipped warm palms beneath his shirt. Groaning at her touch, he dropped his mouth to the column of her neck, his body already aching for her when she whispered, "I want you. I want you. Need you, Cole. Kissing me, touching me, inside me, before we have to…"

It was everything he could do not to haul her into the Chevy's backseat and take her, hot and hard, until she screamed his name. But as desperately as he wanted to give her the release she needed, to take what she had offered, she deserved far better—for far longer—than such a betrayal of the debt of honor he owed her.

Besides, he knew full well that she didn't really mean a single word that she was saying. She was merely acting out, the emotional stress she was under so unbearable that she was willing to do anything—even something he knew she would regret forever—to escape it even for a moment.

Pulling away from her was one of the toughest things he could remember doing, but he damned well wasn't going to lose his chance to save her by giving in to his libido. "I want you, too," he told her honestly, a claim his body's hardness echoed. "Want you so damned bad I'm aching. But I can't. *We* can't—especially not when I need to concentrate on cutting over to that cemetery and casing the surroundings. To concentrate on getting all three of us out of here alive."

"I—I know you're right," she said, and even in the velvety desert darkness, he knew she was crying. "But I hope you'll forgive me if I say I hate you right now for being the voice of reason."

He kissed her one last time, softly on the forehead. "Believe me, Lisa, right now I'd forgive you absolutely anything."

Chapter Fifteen

Lee Ray needed a tweak so bad he couldn't sit still, couldn't rest or eat, though hunger gnawed inside him like a starved wolf. But Evie had only kicked him like a damned dog when he'd asked for more, telling him to get his head straight because he had a job to do. A job he'd freaking better get right if he ever hoped to tweak again.

Standing outside the cabin they had broken into, he shuddered with the biting cold, feeling so twitchy he wanted to pick every square inch of skin bloody, and so furious and frustrated, he needed to pound that bitch's face in. And not the Hartfield bitch, as Evie kept calling Lisa Meador, but Evie herself.

The front door creaked, but it wasn't Evie, as he'd both hoped and dreaded, out to bribe him with a taste or even to scream more threats and insults. Instead, a tiny warm hand slipped inside his cold one. Tyler Meador's hand, followed by that piping voice.

"It's too scary in there with her," he said.

"Get back inside anyway," Lee Ray snapped.

"After the bad people blew up my daddy, I used to get real mad a lot, too. I wanted to hit something, and sometimes I did. But it only made my hand hurt and got me lots of time-outs."

Lee Ray scowled down at him, wanting to tell the brat

to shut up. To stop acting as if they were buddies, and that he'd never been and never could be anybody's daddy.

"My grandpa gave me this special pillow, and he says when the mad gets too big inside me, I should punch it."

"So you punched a pillow," he echoed hollowly. As though he gave a rat's ass.

"I hit it real hard lots of times," Tyler told him, and for the first time, Lee Ray noticed the smudges on the kid's face, along with the griminess of the tattered blanket wrapped around him. He had a runny nose, too. Somebody ought to wipe it.

"I don't need it so much anymore, though," Tyler went on, "so when we get home, you can have it."

"Me?" The boy wanted to give *him* something? Something that had been a present from his grandpa? Lee Ray felt a flicker of warmth in the center of his chest, followed by a stone-cold realization. *Poor little rug rat actually fell for that stupid camping trip story I told him. And he believes he's going home.*

The weight of what he was involved in settled in the icy hollow of his belly, a weight so heavy that he sank to his knees with it. Taking a corner of the ratty blanket, he wiped Tyler's damp nose. But it was only an excuse to lean in close enough to whisper, "Tonight I have to go away for a while," he started, before catching sight of the fear flashing across Tyler's face.

"Don't go! Please! Don't leave me with—"

"Shh," Lee Ray warned. "We can't let her hear us or she'll get mad. We don't want her mad again, do we?"

The boy shook his head quickly, his eyes wide as an owl's, though Lee Ray had so far managed to protect him from the lash of Evie's fury.

"Before me 'n' her take off, we're going to lock you in the cabin," Lee Ray said.

"All by myself?"

Lee Ray nodded, his thoughts coming into a focus so sharp that they surprised him. "Yeah, except—you know that wooden shutter over by the big bunk?"

"What's a shutter?"

"That wooden cover thing over the window. It's coming loose on one side, loose enough that a little guy like you could just squeeze out with your blanket."

"In the dark?" the kid asked, sounding more afraid than ever. Lee Ray wasn't surprised, since the boy had pestered for a night-light till Evie threatened to zip him up inside the duffel and dump it in a black cave, filled with slime and bats and bugs.

"Just think of them stars up there as a million little night-lights. Then you go hide, little dude. You go and hide real good."

"Like for hide-and-seek?" Tyler stared up at him as he spoke, his small voice shaking.

Lee Ray knew the kid was thinking of the canyon's giant boulders, dangerous ravines and thorny thickets, and especially of Evie's "bedtime stories" of giant zombies and bloodthirsty werewolves that would get him if he wandered off alone. But the only monster that scared Lee Ray was Evie herself.

"Yeah," he said. "Only this game has a real good prize."

"What prize?"

Just maybe you get to live. But since Lee Ray couldn't say that, he struggled to come up with some other idea. And something came floating into his memory, something he'd heard Lisa tell the kid to calm him down.

"A medal," he said. "A medal, like for soldiers."

"For real?"

"Oh, yeah. Really real," he lied, starting to sweat, because Evie might come out at any moment.

"My dad got lots of medals before he went to heaven."

Lee Ray felt the breath whoosh out of him, as if he were blowing out a candle. Damn kid was killing him, pushing him to take insane risks. But now that he'd gotten started, he couldn't make himself stop. He'd taken the kid outside earlier to burn off some of his energy and keep him from driving Evie crazy. Because Evie was already plenty crazy at her most sedate. And that memory gave him an idea.

"You remember that old dead tree we played on this afternoon, don'tcha?"

"Uh-huh. The big log that fell down from the mountain. You showed me how to ride it and make it bounce just like a horse."

"Right," Lee Ray said. "I want you to hide down under the end with all the branches, make yourself a little nest in the dry leaves and wait for me. And don't you let her know you're there. No matter what she says, don't you answer her, you hear?"

"And you'll come find me when you get back? Cross your heart and hope to die?"

"Cross my heart," he said, feeling a little silly as he sketched out the gesture. *If I haven't been arrested—or Evie hasn't shot me dead.*

AT TWELVE TWENTY-nine exactly, Lisa pulled into a graveled spot just outside the unfenced graveyard. Her headlights washed over a cluster of tombstones resting among the rocks and scrubby creosote, a final resting place that was a far cry from the green and manicured cemetery where Devin lay buried. Spotting movement, she tensed, her heart slamming its way into her throat.

"Coyote. That's all," she whispered, making out the glowing eyes and shaggy, rail-thin body. As the animal melted away into the darkness, she remembered how to breathe again.

For a moment the sighting made her think about the cougar, a far more dangerous beast. But even if the mountain lion were padding directly toward her, instead of miles away in the Chisos Mountains, she was not about to let fear keep her from doing what she had to do.

Exiting the SUV, she shivered, surprised to realize that the temperature had dropped so low that she could see her breath. But she would be shaking anyway, terrified to imagine that Cole had been spotted as he'd hiked in to scout the perimeter and take up position.

Fighting the temptation to look around for him, she switched on one of the pocket-size flashlights they had picked up at the convenience store, then swung its bright beam toward a pair of twin stone pillars that might once have supported a gate. A cold wind stirred a tumbleweed, which gave a few halfhearted bounces before lodging against a crooked cross.

Out here in the lonely desert, she felt like the last human on the planet. Other than the coyote, she could see no sign of life, only its relics in the form of a pickup parked in front of an old Airstream trailer, a half-collapsed adobe wall and the dark bulk of a few businesses she could not identify.

As she entered the cemetery, her shoulders drew up stiffly, more from nervousness than cold. Every few steps she stopped, her eyes scanning for the slightest flicker, her ears straining for the slightest sound. But she heard nothing but the wind's hiss, the hoot of some small night bird and the low drone of an engine out on Highway 118.

Where are you, Cole? And where is Sabra with my son? Would she even show, or was her demand that Lisa come here no more than a cruel joke? For all she knew, her tormenter was somewhere miles away, meeting the man to whom she'd threatened to sell Tyler. Was her son as cold and scared as she was? As terrified that they would never again see each other?

The disposable phone chirped loudly in her pocket, the sound startling her so badly that she jumped as if she'd been shot. Her own heartbeat like thunder in her ears, she fumbled to answer. But it was just another text, maybe because those messages could come through in places where a regular call couldn't.

Gold star for Daddy's good girl. The venom in those few words drew a shudder. Glad to see you can still follow directions. Now follow these…

"I'm here!" Lisa's voice rang over earth so hard and stony, many of the dead had been laid to rest in above-ground mausoleums. "Now come out. Please, Sabra. Let's talk face-to-face. Let me tell you how very sorry I am for how you suffered. How sorry I am that I was too afraid to get you the help you needed before it was too—"

She stopped speaking abruptly when the phone chimed again, and an instinctive jolt of horror zinged along her spine.

Find the grave of Maria Elena Delgadillo. Climb inside the little fence there.

Little fence, little fence. Flashlight beam dancing frantically before her, Lisa moved as quickly as she could among disordered markers, desperate to spot one surrounded by a fence.

Her mind was screaming what-ifs, each more horrifying than the last. Had Sabra left another set of coordinates, as if she were directing some cruel scavenger hunt?

Worse yet, could she have left Tyler's lifeless body at the grave for her to find?

There—off to the right. Heart in her throat, Lisa approached a fenced plot and confirmed the name on the stone tablet. She noticed the date of Maria Elena Delgadillo's death—exactly eighty years before the December day when Jerry Crowley died and Sabra had gone missing. Beside the tombstone was a small cross, this one reading *Niño,* the Spanish word for "little boy." A little boy lost in infancy, judging from the crudely carved dates.

Lisa hissed as she sliced her hand on the rusty fence when she grabbed it to step inside. Ignoring the bite of pain, she shone the flashlight among the scrubby weeds, but there was no small body, thank God, nothing but some rocks and a few broken liquor bottles.

"There. I've done it," she called, though she had no idea whether Sabra was really close enough to hear her. "Now I need to see my son."

Another chime. Take your clothes off, Sweet Girl Baby, every stitch, and throw them over the fence. Then I want to see you kneel and lean your forehead up against the headstone.

Sweet Girl Baby. It was *definitely* Sabra. Lisa sagged to her knees, tiny bursts of light exploding in her vision. Finally she understood that Cole had been right about this from the outset. Trying to placate a psychopath was like chasing shadows.

No matter what she did, there would be no end to the torments Sabra inflicted on her. The woman meant to humiliate and torture her for as many hours as it took to utterly break her down, having obviously grown obsessed with destroying her. And then Sabra would shoot her— or maybe bash her head in, just as she had promised so many years before.

The cruel voice floated into her mind from the distant past. *"I've never backed off from a threat. Not ever."*

Apparently that was true even if it took her twenty years to follow through. And even worse, once it was over, the same evil creature who had once crushed baby birds with her shoes would only laugh off her promise to spare Tyler anyway.

Inside Lisa, a wall crashed down as she realized that out here, in this time and place, the rules that guided the civilized, the sane, no longer held sway.

Now that Cole's eyes had adjusted, he could see far more than he had been able to at first. The moon's absence, along with the lack of light pollution, drew out the hazy band of the Milky Way, which offered just enough illumination for an experienced night hunter to get by on. And get by he did, squatting on a low rise, listening to Lisa calling to Evie and keeping the bright star of her flashlight in his peripheral vision at all times.

Mostly, though, he was scanning the darkness all around her, his gaze sweeping from the tombstones to the rocky gateposts and more distant pickup—anything that could hide a human figure.

There. He had one of them in his sights. He couldn't yet tell which, couldn't even be a hundred percent certain he wasn't looking at a stray dog or one of the piglike native javelinas.

No, he realized as the shadow shifted. The figure might be hunching low, looking through an empty window in a crumbling wall that was all that remained of what had once been an adobe house perched just above the cemetery, but it was definitely two-legged. And not necessarily alone.

Figuring the watcher would be focusing on Lisa, he

crept closer, Lisa's gun in hand, an arrangement she'd agreed to after admitting that she'd never actually fired a weapon. Somehow he had to make his way to that wall without being spotted, then silently subdue his target, so he could find out where they had stashed Tyler.

The trouble was, he needed to slip up behind his quarry, but that meant he would no longer be able to watch for the muzzle of a weapon aimed at Lisa, no longer be able to so much as shout out a warning for her to duck.

Somewhere not far away a coyote's solitary yip touched off an answering chorus. A moment later Lisa's voice rose above the din, her words clipped and furious instead of fearful.

"I came here alone just like you wanted. I came for my son, 'Evie.'" She spat out the alias with obvious disgust. "If you've got the guts to crawl out of your hidey-hole to talk, then come and get me. But I'm finished playing your twisted little text-the-patsy game, you sadistic bitch."

What the hell? After insisting on following the kidnapper's demands to the letter, was Lisa trying to get herself killed? Adrenaline surging through his veins, Cole raced up the back of the hill, toward the wall—and prayed that Lisa's challenge would provide enough of a distraction that the watcher wouldn't see or hear him coming.

Suddenly someone moved out from behind the wall and started scrambling downhill, cursing in a male voice with each step. Cole chose a course to intercept him.

"Don't you do it, Evie," the man said, leaving Cole uncertain whether he was talking into a phone or to himself. "Don't you dump me here to go 'n' kill that kid. Don't you—"

An angry burst of automatic gunfire interrupted his words. And it came from the cemetery below.

Chapter Sixteen

As bullets ricocheted off tombstones, fence and rocks alike, Lisa threw herself to the ground, biting down on her tongue as she fought not to scream.

The shooting stopped abruptly, and the world fell deathly silent. So silent, and for so long, that her nerves stretched to the breaking point as she wondered, would the next bullet kill her? Or had Sabra left already, rushing to take out Lisa's defiance on her son?

Finally she heard the light crunch of approaching footsteps on the gravel. Had Cole come to find her?

But the words that floated from the darkness were chiseled out of ice.

"Sabra's dead because of *you*," said Evie. "Just like the lady in the grave and her dead whelp. Just like me and mine and you and yours."

Wanting to cry and plead, to shout and rage at this new threat, Lisa fought to hold back the floodgates on her emotions. "I don't understand," she said, tears pushing through as she clambered to her feet. "If Sabra's really dead, who *are* you? Why are you doing this to my son and me?"

"She was so strong. She was invincible—practically a goddess in that crappy little town—until you blabbed."

"What?" Lisa blinked as the pieces snapped together,

like the bonds of sisterhood. Twisted bonds, in this case. "Are you *Ava?* Ava Crowley? Why would you—"

From somewhere outside the cemetery, a male voice shouted, "Watch out! He's coming at us!"

A pop of gunfire followed, two quick shots before Evie whirled to shoot toward the sound. Springing to her feet, Lisa stepped over the fence, her every instinct screaming to run to the relative safety of her rental.

Instead, she rushed after Evie, desperately launching herself at the taller woman from behind, needing at all costs to stop her before she killed Cole, to subdue her and force her to give up Tyler's location.

The impact sent them both crashing to the ground, with Lisa slamming down on top of Evie—or Ava, if that was really who she was. As the woman fought to flip her over and regain control of the weapon pinned beneath her, Lisa reached under her for the gun, screaming into her ear, "Let go!" Finally she wrapped her hand around some part of the automatic.

Her palm and fingers burning, Lisa realized she had grabbed the still-hot barrel. But she didn't dare let go, though Evie swore and elbowed, fighting like a demon.

When Evie's teeth sank into her forearm, Lisa shrieked with pain, shock making her hand reflexively release.

As Evie struggled to her feet, Cole yelled from somewhere nearby, "Move away from her—now!"

"Watch out!" Lisa cried. "She still has the—"

Then something struck her hard in the head, a kick that brought the stars down with a sound like breaking glass.

Sometimes, in the heat of the moment, a man could take a bullet and barely even notice.

It hadn't been like that for Cole this time. He'd felt the burn of the bullet in his left thigh when the man he'd been trailing had suddenly wheeled around and fired. Pure dumb luck on the shooter's part—and one of the hazards of trying to take a man alive.

But the explosion of pain that was the price of each step hadn't stopped him. Nor had he quit advancing, only ducked behind any monument tall enough to offer shelter, when Evie fired in his direction, one of her bullets striking her own partner, who cried out before collapsing.

He'd been driven by the need to get to Lisa, to save her before Evie could—

He shouted to Evie to get away from Lisa, then heard Lisa call out a truncated warning. His stomach pitched wildly with the thought that he might already be too late, that those could have been the last words she ever spoke.

No. He wouldn't let her die, even if he had to take another bullet.

Ahead, he heard the sound of panting and the clatter of small rocks. Evie, on the move, rushing away from him. Away from Lisa, too.

Unless she was taking Lisa with her.

No, she couldn't be. He'd clearly heard only one person running, leaving Lisa behind, as silent as the dead. Or maybe she was playing possum?

He couldn't allow himself to wonder. Couldn't let himself feel. Yet it felt like something from a dream, stopping to reach for the fallen man's gun, his own muscles tensing with the pain ripping through his damaged thigh.

The hand that gripped the weapon tightened, the tattooed man's hoarse murmur reaching his ears. "Help me. Hurts so…bad. My guts—they're all on fire."

"Where's the boy?" Cole demanded. "If you want your miserable life to count for anything…"

Grimacing, the man choked out, "Yeah…you gotta find the kid before she gets there. Or she'll k-kill him for sure."

"Where? Where is he?"

"Hiding." A bubbling cough was followed by a deep moan.

"Hiding where?" Cole grabbed his shoulder, shook him. "Where?"

"Fa-fallen treetop, slanting down into the canyon. Maybe a-a couple hundred yards out from the cabin."

Alarm sliced through Cole. There had to be scores, perhaps hundreds, of canyons in the area. It would take years to search them all. Time that Tyler didn't have. "Which canyon? Tell me, or so help me…"

But the threat was clearly pointless. The wounded man clearly didn't have long.

"Your girlfriend was the one," Cole said. "She's the one who did this to you, not me."

"Always knew that Evie'd get me." This time the moan was longer, softer, and the man's voice faltered as he struggled to continue. "One way or the other."

"But you care about the boy, right? You don't want her to hurt him. So tell me, damn it. Before it's too late."

He leaned near the man's mouth, struggling to hear what he was saying. The sound was nearly drowned out as a nearby engine roared to life. Rising, Cole made out a pair of taillights, what looked like the stolen Explorer heading toward 118.

Cole heard footsteps. Uneven and stumbling, a flashlight beam bouncing ahead of them.

Relief swelled in his chest, sending rivers of warmth through him. "Lisa? Lisa, are you all right?"

"Cole! Where are you?"

"Right here." He bent and felt for the accomplice's carotid. And found not even the flicker of a pulse.

Grimacing, he straightened, then limped to meet her

and clasped her to him. Stroking her hair, he warned, "Don't look."

But she must have seen the dead man in the beam of her flashlight, because a moment later he heard her gasp.

"It's him—I know those tattoos," she said. "He was with her. Did you…?"

"No. Evie shot him. What about you? Are you all right?"

"Nasty headache where she kicked me, but I'll be fine. But Tyler," Lisa said. "I have to find my son."

"Let's move," Cole said.

Swallowing hard against the flaring agony in his leg, he struggled to keep up with her.

Before long, she paused to look back his way, her flashlight skimming him. "Your leg. Oh, Cole. She hit you, too."

"Not her—the guy. But it's nothing serious," he said, praying it was true. He felt damp heat and the sticky sensation of his pant leg plastered to the skin with blood. How much blood, he couldn't be sure, but he would've gone down already if the bullet had nicked an artery.

"Are you sure you can keep—"

"There's no choice," he said. "We have to find Tyler before she does."

By the time they reached the SUV, there was no sign of Evie's taillights.

"Hop in," he told Lisa. "I'm driving."

"With a bullet in you?"

"I'm pretty sure you've got a concussion, and that trumps my bullet wound. She kicked you in the head, right? Are you even seeing straight?"

He took it as confirmation that she wasn't when she dug into her pocket and then handed him the key. He climbed into the SUV, biting back a groan. At least the wound was on his left side, so he would be able to work the gas and the brakes.

"Should we try to bandage that?" she asked, looking around the vehicle. "I threw an extra shirt in my bag. Maybe we could at least wad it up and—"

"No time for that." He fired up the engine. "And really, it's not that bad."

"Did you see which way she went?" she asked.

"The general direction, yeah. And I know for sure she's heading back toward the park."

"How?" she asked.

"Tattooed guy grew a conscience." He backed up, turning around. "Too bad he waited till his last breath to use it."

"Did he—did he say that Tyler's still alive?"

"He seemed to think he was. Wanted us to get to him before Evie could."

"What did he say?" Lisa demanded.

Cole told her what little he knew as they roared toward the highway, stones spewing from beneath their wheels.

"He was right about Evie." Lisa's voice sounded strained to the breaking point. "She does mean to kill Tyler. She wants to get back at me."

"What happened down there? Why did you yell at her?"

"Her last texts made it very clear that no amount of playing her game was ever going to change things. She's meant to kill me all along —and Tyler, too. I doubt there's ever even been a mystery pervert who wanted to buy him. I think Ava only said that to freak me out."

"Ava? Sabra's sister? Wait a minute. I thought you were convinced we've been dealing with Sabra herself."

"She blames me for Sabra's death. She told me that much just before I jumped her."

"You *jumped* her?"

"She was shooting at you. I couldn't let her—"

"Thank you," he said, humbled that she had tried to protect him armed with nothing but her bare hands. "You could have been killed."

"I'd rather die on my terms than go down without a fight."

"You're not going down at all, Lisa, not if I can help it," Cole swore. "And we're going to save Tyler. We're finding him tonight."

SOLDIERS WENT ON CAMPOUTS. Tyler's grandpa had told him that once, the night he'd set up the tent in the backyard for them to sleep in.

It was after Daddy had died, and Grandpa was in town trying to make him feel better. But even with Grandpa on the air mattress beside him, the darkness had been kind of scary and a few tears sneaked out, not like real crying, but almost.

Then Mommy had brought out s'mores, and Grandpa started telling stories. And they'd talked about his dad, and Mom had started smiling, telling about how he'd hidden a hurt dog in his tent once, even though the officers might have sent him to the principal if he was caught.

But Daddy wasn't scared, and he had decided he wouldn't be, either—not even when Grandpa's snoring sounded just like bear growls and Rowdy peed on the sleeping bag a little 'cause he was just a baby puppy back then.

Tonight, though, Grandpa wasn't here, and Rowdy wasn't, either. But Tyler had pushed his octopus out through the window, and the sleeping bag, too, because it wouldn't be a real campout without them.

Then he'd taken the blanket, as the Picture Man had

told him, 'cause it was real cold in the cabin, so it would be even colder outside.

Before squeezing himself out, too, Tyler had stopped and put his hand over his tummy. It hurt and felt all squishy, as if he might have to throw up. He wondered if he would have to fall far when he went out the window.

And what if the mean lady was out there, waiting for him to "try something"? That was what she always said. *"If you try something, you'll be sorry."*

His stomach hurt worse, thinking of her, so he thought about his mom instead. His mom, with her arms out to catch him, to wrap him in the best hug ever.

But it was Picture Man's voice he heard, leaning over, saying, *"Just think of them stars up there as a million little night-lights. Then you go hide, little dude. You go and hide real good."*

Chapter Seventeen

LeStrange, LeStage. The two names weren't so very different. In light of the conversation Jill Keller had had with Sheriff Stewart, she couldn't believe that no one had figured out the woman's identity sooner, based on the surname she and her sister had been born with.

But then, if Lisa Meador's father hadn't called her boss, who would have thought to look into such an old crime, let alone one rooted in another county? If anyone—if she herself—had only thought to dig so far back, surely this case could have been solved so much sooner. And with a far less bloody outcome than the one she was expecting.

Make that dreading, Jill amended as she took a turn toward Terlingua. She quickly spotted several vehicles, their headlights flooding the cemetery as three men gathered around what she prayed would not prove to be Lisa or Tyler Meador's body, or Cole Sawyer's.

She pulled up and jumped from the car, staring in confusion at the bearded man coming toward her waving his arms. Maybe six-four and two hundred thirty pounds, he still managed to look more shaken up than dangerous.

"You from the sheriff's office?" he asked, nodding toward her badge and uniform. "We've got a dead fella down there. Shot straight through the belly."

She shook her head and explained, "I'm from Tuller County in central Texas. What happened here, sir?"

"Heard some kind of shoot-out from my trailer." He nodded toward an ancient Airstream. "Peeked out my window and saw a woman and a man take off after another vehicle. Soon as we were sure the shooting was all over, me and my neighbors came over here and found him, but he was dead, all right."

"What were these people driving?"

"Too dark to make out colors, but they both looked like SUVs. The couple's might've been a Chevy."

Perfect, Jill thought, rooting for the same couple she had earlier suspected, now that Sheriff Stewart had put things into perspective—and given her a royal chewing-out. "So, who's the victim?"

The man shook his shaggy head, then pulled a folded scrap of paper from the pocket of his flannel shirt. "No ID, but he's pretty inked up. And he had this in his pocket."

Taking it, she carefully unfolded the scrap. Despite the blood that had soaked into one corner, she smiled at what she saw.

AHEAD AND TO THE right, a flash of red lights punctured the darkness like two fang wounds.

"Right there. That's her, isn't it?" Lisa's pulse leaped as she pointed, but before she had the words out, the tail-lights vanished.

Had she been staring into the darkness, hoping, for so long that she'd only dreamed them? Or did the two spots have more to do with her pounding head and swimming vision?

"I saw them, too," Cole confirmed. "She must've crested another hill."

A half hour earlier they had followed a solitary set of

lights onto a turnoff that led into the Chisos Mountains, according to a road sign. Dark as it was, Lisa felt the inclines becoming steeper and the curves growing more frequent. She made out darker chunks of night, too, starless silhouettes of rock looming high above them.

"Drive faster, Cole. We have to catch her," she urged.

"We follow too close and she'll see us coming, then try to ambush us again or lead us on some wild-goose chase." His voice came out a frustrated growl. "Would've been a lot simpler if that guy had given me the canyon's name before he died instead of just a vague description of where Tyler might be hiding. Then we could call for backup and directions."

"Not on either one of these phones," Lisa told him. No longer caring if the FBI traced them, she had replaced the battery in Cole's cell. But, like the disposable Evie had sent her, it had no signal in this remote terrain.

"Keep checking," Cole urged. "Meanwhile, use my phone to text your father. Maybe you can get that through, at least. Tell him to call the authorities and let him know we're in the park, somewhere in the Chisos Mountains."

"What's the name of this road?"

He quickly rattled off the route number.

Lisa painstakingly composed the text, cursing the way the words kept doubling on the lit screen and the pitching of her stomach with each curve in the road.

She pushed Send and waited, but the message sat like a brick in the phone's out-box. "It's not working."

"Just leave the phone on," he said. "It'll keep trying automatically, in case we pick up a signal."

"Not much chance of a cell tower out here, is there?"

"Might be one because of the park, but it's hard to say, with all this rock to block the signals. We may be on our own here."

She swallowed, her throat burning as if she'd downed a live coal. So it would just be the two of them, poorly armed, both injured and neither of them knowing exactly where they were going.

"Then we'll have to be enough," she said. "Because I haven't come this far to let her—"

He reached over, touching her arm. "You mean *we* haven't, Lisa. Because I damned well mean to see this through."

"For my husband's sake." She blinked back tears, her face heating with the memory of how she'd forgotten Devin, God forgive her, to throw herself at the man who'd failed to save him.

Cole shook his head. "There's no paying back debts owed the dead. I'm doing this for *you,* for you and Tyler both."

"But you don't even know us, not really."

He spared her a brief glance. "That's where you're wrong. I know *you,* at least. Out here, this is warfare. There's no time for small talk, nowhere to hide your true self. I've seen you stripped naked, Lisa. Naked to your soul."

There was a dizzy moment of stunned silence as she struggled to process his words, to fight off the images that tumbled through her pounding head. Images of the two of them, naked not in soul but body. Images that mocked the vows she'd made to the man he'd failed to save.

"And I like what I see," Cole said, his voice rough with something that sounded like pure masculine desire, despite the way he had turned her aside before.

"You're not only beautiful, but you're kind," he continued, "yet you'd claw the eyes out of anybody who threatens those you love. And even me, though heaven knows you've got every reason in the world to hate me. You don't sit back and wait for help. You have the guts to take on challenges, no matter how tough."

She shook her head, feeling like a fraud. Couldn't he see how terrified she was, how scared she'd been her whole life of bullies like Sabra Crowley, of being on her own? She might do what she had to, pretending to be grown-up, but deep inside she was still that little girl shivering beneath the covers between her mom and dad.

"No matter how hard I tried to tell myself that helping you and Tyler was just an obligation," Cole said, "that's not the way I feel anymore. It's not who I am. Because I've come to care about you, Lisa. And I care about your son because you love him."

She wanted to say something, at the very least to admit how deeply his words touched her. But things were going too fast, spinning too far out of control. *She'd* been out of control before, saying things she didn't mean, just as Cole was now. And this time it was up to her to stop it before he went any further…or, worse yet, she allowed herself to believe.

Besides, some still-raw corner of her psyche whispered, *what if Cole's hurt worse than he's saying? What if he dies on you, like Devin?*

Her heart plummeted at the thought. Terrified as she was for Tyler, she couldn't let herself become any more emotionally involved with this man. Couldn't take the risk.

So instead she said simply, "Thank you," as if in risking his life, risking his emotions, he was deserving of no more gratitude than a passing stranger holding a door open.

Afterward they both grew quiet, except to comment on several signs pointing out the way to specific peaks or trailheads. Eventually Cole took a right turn, following the taillights onto a rutted, unpaved road with one final marker reading Now Leaving Big Bend National Park.

Steadily the track led downward, its roughness forcing him to slow. Eventually they rolled to a stop. "Are you seeing anything?" he asked. "Any sign of her lights?"

"Not for a while. You think maybe she turned off somewhere?" Her stomach pitched at the thought of how easy it would be to miss a turn in this inky blackness.

"Either that or she might've pulled over and shut off her lights to wait for us to pass." Cole lowered the windows, and turned off the lights and engine.

"What are you doing?" Anxiety wound tight inside her, because every moment that they sat there was giving Evie more time to find Tyler.

"Just listen," he whispered, reaching up to disable the dome light. "Listen and look, with no distractions."

Within the dark and silent bubble, her fear was the distraction. Her heart was pounding so hard that she was surprised Cole couldn't hear it. "Please…"

He didn't answer, but she swore she could feel him just beside her, his senses straining for the slightest flicker, or the sound of any— *There.* "I heard something," she whispered, then pointed off ahead and to the left. "A car door closing, over that way."

He grasped her hand and squeezed it, silently communicating that she should keep still. Lacing her fingers through his, she willed herself to trust him, though her body was vibrating with the need for action.

"Over there," he said softly, lifting her hand toward a suffused glow, a light so faint they surely would have missed it had they kept driving. "That must be the cabin. I'd better get out now and cut through these trees. Otherwise she'll hear us coming."

"What if she finds Tyler before we do?"

"He's hiding, remember? And I'll be quick, I promise."

"I'm coming with you," she said, thinking of stories she'd heard about children perishing in house fires because they hid from the firefighters there to save them. "Tyler doesn't know you. He could be frightened by a strange man."

"All right. But if I tell you to duck, you do it. If I tell you to go back, you run and find help." He pressed the SUV keys in her hand.

Turned around as she was, she couldn't imagine where she would drive for help. Nor could she fathom the idea of leaving him and Tyler, regardless of what happened.

"Let's go," she answered, stepping out of the car.

He came around to get her, taking her by the arm. "Stick right by me," he ordered, "and leave that flashlight in your pocket, in case we need it later. For now, though, the darkness is our one advantage," he said. "We can't give it away."

It might be an advantage for him, but Lisa felt like a blind woman, led by her sighted guide. She wondered if his ability was borne of Ranger training and experience, or if those storm-gray eyes of his had always sliced through darkness as keenly as an owl's.

As keenly, she remembered, as he claimed to see through her. *"I've seen you stripped naked, Lisa. Naked to your soul."*

She shivered at the thought, struggling to keep up with the man whose stealth and speed seemed almost unnatural, despite his injury. Unlike her, he never snapped a stick or stubbed his toe against a rock. And when she stumbled into a low spot and pitched forward, he managed to catch her before she crashed onto her knees.

"Sorry," she whispered, in response to the low groan that told her what the sudden move had cost him. Swallowing her pride, she managed, "I really am slowing you down, aren't I?"

Beside her, she felt him go still. An instant later a sound registered, a noise that started low, then swelled to a cry as tortured as a woman's dying scream.

Instinctively, Lisa recoiled, every fine hair on her body rising, because as human as it sounded, she understood that it wasn't. That it was a sound as native to this wilderness as she and Cole and Tyler, even Ava, were alien.

"We have to keep moving," Cole said quietly. "Noises like that echo off the rock and carry. It's not nearly as close as it sounds."

"What *is* it?" she asked, her skin crawling with suspicion.

"Mountain lion," he confirmed. "Probably miles away. And more than likely not the same cat that—"

"I've held you back long enough," she said, in no mood to be placated. "Leave me here and go find Tyler. Find my son before someone or something gets to him first."

A NOISE WOKE TYLER from a deep sleep, a scary noise that started him thinking about the monsters from the mean lady's mean stories. His heart pounded, and he shivered in his sleeping bag, hating this night even more than the others. He wanted his own bed, in his own house, more than ever. Wanted Rowdy curled up beside him, and his mom to snuggle him and read him stories until they all fell asleep in one big, cozy pile with Octobuddy squished right in the middle.

He felt all around him in the sleeping bag, in the crumpled wad of blanket, even in the scratchy, poky sticks and needles all around him. But he couldn't find it anywhere. His octopus was gone.

Maybe he'd dropped him on the way here, or forgotten him when he cut his knee falling out the window. But either way, now Octobuddy was lost, too. All by himself, out there somewhere in the big, cold, dark outside.

Tyler started sniffling as he remembered how his mom had told him that his octopus and Rowdy were his troops, and he needed to keep them from getting scared. And now he'd lost them both. What kind of soldier did that make him?

Wondering what his dad would do, he thought about a rescue mission. He could find his lost friend and get extra medals 'cause he'd be a real live hero. The idea made him so excited that he slipped out of his sleeping bag and started back in the direction he'd come.

At least he thought it was the right direction. He stopped a few steps later, squinting hard into the darkness, and then changed course. After a few more steps, he stopped again, feeling mixed up with the weird shadows that looked more frightening than any monster.

He shivered, rubbing his arms and wishing he'd remembered to bring his blanket with him. But a good soldier never left a man behind, so Tyler started marching, moving fast so he could keep warm.

Moving so fast, there was no warning when the whole world dropped away.

IF THE INCIDENT IN Lashkar Gah had taught Cole nothing else, it was that a moment's hesitation could have deadly consequences. Consequences that he damned well didn't want to live with.

"You take this one," he said, passing her the .22. "It's lighter and easier to use than the extra I picked up."

"But I really don't know how to—"

"Safety's off, so be careful. But if you have to shoot,

aim for the center of the chest and pull the trigger. However many times it takes."

"Cole…" she said. "I just want to tell you that I—"

His cool fingers touched her cheek. "Back to the car, Lisa. But after I bring Tyler, we'll talk. After this is over, I promise."

Hard as it was to leave her, he forced himself to move out at a more rapid clip. Praying that the big cat's call really was as distant as he'd claimed, he put it out of mind, focusing like a laser on the sound of the car door and the flicker of light he'd made out earlier.

The harder he pushed himself, the harder the pain pushed back. Fatigue, too, probably a result of blood loss. But he had learned the difference between what his body thought it could do and what it *actually* could, so with an iron will, he kept pressing, moving into a jog that forced him to pay careful attention to his footing on the uneven ground as he scanned his surroundings, looking for either the cabin or the fallen tree the tattooed accomplice had described.

Soon a new sound had him stopping short, his hot breath fogging the air before him. Car engine, he realized, glancing back toward the dirt road. Could Lisa have made it back to the SUV already? And if so, why would she risk the noise?

A wave of dizziness washed over him, his body's warning that he was closer to his limits than he'd thought. Flurries of white spots clouded his vision, nonexistent snow that melted away when he blinked.

As his eyes cleared, his stomach lurched as he saw that he'd stopped only one short step from disaster. Just ahead lay a steep drop-off—a dark space he'd mistaken for a band of shadow.

It was a ravine, long and narrow, blocking him from

the spot where he'd heard Ava's vehicle—a spot she might have left already while he'd wasted time attempting to cut through these woods to catch her unaware. The question was, should he try to press forward or get back to Lisa as fast as possible?

Peering over the precipice, he tried to gauge the ravine's depth. Unable to see the bottom in the dark, he kicked a small stone over the edge instead. He heard its tumbling clatter, soft clicks as it struck one rock after another, followed by a sharp—and very human—cry.

Chapter Eighteen

Lisa gasped as she tripped, scraping her palm painfully against a thorny shrub. But she was determined not to end up in need of rescue herself, so she pushed herself to her feet and forced herself to move more slowly.

She shivered with the cold, her stomach knotting as she worried that Cole would arrive too late to find Tyler, that that horrible, sick woman had already—

No. She couldn't, *wouldn't,* think it, nor could she think about the mountain lion that had killed that female hiker. But even so, the realization pressed in on her that up here in these mountains, she was on the big cat's turf and not her own. And so was Tyler, even if he managed to remain hidden from Ava.

Lisa froze, hearing something. A soft voice from the direction of the dirt road where they had left the SUV. A voice she would know anywhere, an answer to her prayers.

"Tyler!" she cried, racing in the direction of the sound. Tears of joy and relief burned her eyes, choking her as she ran.

As she broke from the cover of the trees, she saw she'd overshot the rental. Though she was about fifty yards ahead of it, she could see it clearly, because the dome light was on and the passenger-side door stood open.

How could Cole have gotten back already? Or had

Tyler spotted the Chevy from his hiding place and made it there on his own?

"Tyler!" she called again. "Tyler, honey."

Though she saw no movement, she heard the same words that had drawn her originally.

"Hurry, Mommy. Hurry, please!"

The same words.

The same cadence.

The exact same intonation, all of it chillingly familiar.

She stopped in her tracks, staring at her rental, only about twenty yards ahead now. Without warning, the high beams came on, and she raised her arm, protecting her eyes from the blinding blast of light.

"Cole?" she called, her voice trembling. "Tyler?"

Squinting, she made out a familiar object only a few feet ahead.

It was Tyler's stuffed octopus, crumpled and forlorn. A lump forming in her throat, Lisa stepped forward to claim it.

"HELLO?" COLE called, his heart pounding and every muscle tensed with expectation. Had it been real, the cry he'd heard, or only the product of a desperate wish? Or maybe it had been some animal hit by the stone, and his imagination had led him to hear it as human.

A hoarse sob rose from the ravine, a raw-throated cry that was definitely human—a child in distress.

Pulling out his flashlight, Cole risked turning it on and calling, "Tyler? Tyler Meador, can you hear me? Your mom sent me to help you. Are you hurt?"

There was no answer beyond the boy's continuing cries. Cries that sounded so close that Cole painfully lowered himself to his stomach, then hung his arm and flashlight over the rim. Praying for all he was worth, he swept the beam downward, skimming the rocky wall beneath him.

And stopping at a splash of color—the grimy pale blue T-shirt of a tiny figure curled and shivering on a narrow ledge of rock about twenty feet below. And just beyond, a deeper crack so black and fathomless, it made Cole's stomach pitch to see it.

Whether Tyler had been thrown off this ledge or had fallen on his own, he had landed only inches from what would very likely be a fatal drop.

"Cold," the boy said, tears streaming down his face. "I'm cold. And I want Mommy."

"Your mom's in the car. There's a nice warm heater there, too. And Rowdy's waiting for you at home. He can't wait to—"

"Rowdy's lost. The mean lady made the Picture Man push him out of the car 'cause he growled and tried to bite her."

Cole made a mental note to buy the little fluff ball a filet mignon next time he saw him. "Your mom and I found your dog," he said as he peeled off his coat. "Just like we found you. Tell me, Tyler, are you hurt?"

"My arm hurts, and my knee, too. Can you put some Band-Aids on them and make them all better?"

Cole's heart twisted, touched by the boy's willingness to trust in spite of everything he'd been through.

"I'm Captain Sawyer, Tyler, and I'm going to do my very best to help you," he said, "but it might take me a few minutes to get down to you. So I'm going to drop my jacket first. I want you to try to catch it, but if it's too far out, just let it go. All right?"

The last thing he wanted to do was send Tyler over the edge, so he aimed carefully before letting the jacket drop.

"Great catch, champ," Cole said, when it landed across

the child's outstretched arm. "Now I want you to wrap yourself up in it, just like a superhero's cape. Can you do that?"

Tyler did so, then looked up at him. "How come it's wet and yucky on the bottom?"

"Must've dragged it through a puddle." No reason to scare the kid any more than he already was by admitting that the "yuckiness" was his own blood.

Nor did Cole want to risk leaving the little guy alone, with Evie—or Ava—still potentially out here somewhere. Even so, the climb down could still prove deadly if he accidentally sent a loose rock tumbling down onto the boy.

Better to move off to the right and begin his descent there, then try to sidestep his way over. Difficult, in his condition, but not impossible.

"I'm coming down to get you," Cole said, fighting past both pain and dizziness to move into what he judged to be the optimum position. And drawing strength from a vision, glowing and ethereal, of the beautiful Lisa Meador reunited with her son.

"Hurry, Mommy! Hurry, please!"

Lisa blinked as Ava stepped out from a clump of trees, smiling cruelly as she raised the smartphone she was holding in one hand.

"I just love these little gizmos, don't you?" she said as she replayed the recorded message yet again. "And I like these even better," she added, jerking the muzzle of the AK-47 higher.

"Where's my son?" Lisa managed, her legs weakening beneath her. "What have you done with him, you coldhearted bitch?"

"What do you think I did with him? I came straight back here and cut the brat's throat in his sleep."

"No," Lisa groaned, squeezing her son's toy tight. And noticing for the first time the smear of blood on one of the stuffed tentacles.

Dropping to her knees, she hunched forward, sobbing, her heart splintering into pieces. After she'd fought so hard, risked so much, to get him back, to find that this woman had murdered something so sweet and so precious… Now her only child, her entire reason for living, was gone, and for what? Some twisted form of revenge for some imagined slight to a woman's sister two decades before?

But what did it matter now, with Tyler gone? What did any of it matter?

"Don't cry for him, Sweet Girl Baby," Ava told her brightly as she bent low enough to stroke Lisa's hair. "You won't have long to miss him. You'll be joining your son and your dear husband very soon."

PAIN BURNING THROUGH HIS thigh with every hard-won inch, Cole fought his way downward, handhold by precarious handhold. Cold as it was, sweat poured off his body, and occasionally he had to rest until the spots cleared from his vision. But each time the thought of reuniting Tyler with his mother infused him with a strength he had never felt before.

Because for all the times you've risked your life for your compatriots, your duty and your country's honor, you've never before done it for someone you love.

Love? The notion made the darkness spin around him, a darkness heavy with the immensity of what he dared to feel for Devin Meador's widow. But wrong as it was, he couldn't spare the energy to deny what he felt.

"How much longer?" Tyler asked, sounding small and cold and frightened.

"Almost there," Cole said. "Just one more big step and—"

"Hello? Cole Sawyer?"

Startled by the female voice above them, Cole looked up into a blinding beam of light. At the same moment his weight settled on the flat rock where Tyler waited.

A rock that abruptly tilted as his weight came to rest on it.

At Tyler's scream, Cole jerked back with a shout of alarm and desperately grabbed for a rock or root—anything that would keep him from plunging to his death.

"Hold on, Tyler!" Jill Keller cried, because Cole Sawyer's fall had left the child, too, crying out, scrambling for purchase.

"Don't let me fall!" the boy screamed as a jacket slid off his shoulders, slipping into the depths.

Just as Tyler would soon slip, with the rock supporting him slowly but inevitably giving way. Heart pounding out a frantic rhythm, Jill knew that if she attempted to climb down to him, she could easily be killed, too. Or get stuck in this cold pit where no one might find her for days or even weeks. And the woman who had nearly killed Trace, the woman Jill had come so far, so fast to repay, would slip from her grasp forever.

"Sawyer?" she called. "Cole Sawyer, this is Deputy Jill Keller. Can you hear me?"

She heard nothing but the small boy's crying. Not another sound.

"Lisa Meador?" she tried. "Lisa, are you down there?"

Hearing no answer, she asked, "Tyler, where's your mama?"

Tyler stopped crying for a moment. "In the car. She's waiting for me with the heater."

Jill's heart sank, because she'd passed Lisa's SUV on the way here. There had been no one inside it, no sign of life at all. Had "Evie LeStrange" killed her, or was she out searching for her lost child somewhere in this deadly darkness?

"Please, come get me," Tyler called up to her. "Please take me to my mommy!"

And in a child's desperation, Jill felt something shift within her soul. Felt the dawning awareness that, as Lisa Meador and Cole Sawyer had both proven, there *were* some things worth risking death for.

How could she have wasted so much of her life believing that anger and revenge, let alone ambition, had ever been among them?

GRIEF'S BLACK CURTAIN PARTED, and all that Lisa saw beyond it was the bright bloodred of fury. So Ava wanted vengeance for her sister? Well, that sword sliced both ways.

Especially when this particular "victim" had not a damned thing left to lose.

"On your feet and in the car," her captor ordered, grabbing Lisa by the arm.

But leaving her right hand free to dive into the pocket of her jacket with a speed and surety Lisa would never have dreamed she possessed.

As nonviolent and law-abiding as she'd been her whole life, she had no intention of subduing, or even wounding, Ava Crowley. She wanted, *needed,* to put down the woman who had taken Tyler from her like the mad dog that she was.

Insane as she was, Ava must have had a sixth sense, because she jerked Lisa by the hair, throwing her off balance. Instinctively moving to catch herself as she fell back to the ground, Lisa still managed to squeeze off one wild shot before Ava stomped on her hand, then snatched away the weapon and shoved it into the pocket of the cargo pants that she was wearing.

"Nice try—if you were aiming for my toes," she said, her cruel laughter ringing off the nearby rocks. "Now get in the car, bitch, and I'll take you to a nice, quiet spot where I can show you how it's done."

ABOVE HIM, COLE heard Tyler crying, but he didn't have the energy to tell the boy that he was coming. To tell him he would scale the gates of hell itself if that was what it took. Instead, he pulled himself upward using the branches of the fallen tree he'd managed to catch on his way down, every muscle straining, every tendon standing out.

Deputy Keller called his name, but he couldn't answer her, either, much less ask her what she was doing five hundred miles outside her jurisdiction, apparently alone. Remembering the wild look in her eyes the night her partner had been injured, he suspected she had gone rogue, which made her a dangerously unpredictable ally.

Climbing sideways, hand-over-hand, Cole found the going even tougher. Every time he attempted to edge toward Tyler, the rock gave way, no matter how carefully he moved.

"Just hold on a minute," he heard the deputy call. "I'm coming for you, Tyler. So whatever you do, don't let go."

From somewhere beyond the ravine, a crack echoed through the darkness. A shot that sounded as though it might have come from Lisa's .22.

Adrenaline ripping through him, he tried to convince himself that as inexperienced as she was with firearms, she might have started at some sound or shadow and accidentally squeezed off a shot. But no matter how hard he tried, he couldn't make himself believe she would risk the noise unless she'd absolutely had to.

Which meant he had to get to her as fast as he could, but how could he leave Tyler in danger?

He managed to draw breath and call, "Deputy, did you hear that?"

"Sawyer," she replied, sounding out of breath herself. "Glad to know you're still among the living, but I'm a little…distracted right now."

He heard the light rain of pebbles that marked her progress.

"You still with me, Tyler?" she asked, her focus clearly on the boy. "No! Don't try to come to me, sweetheart. I'll be there in just a minute."

"Listen to her, Tyler," Cole urged, his gut twisting with his tension. "I can't get over to you, so I'm heading up to get your mom." *If she's still alive.*

"Careful up there," the deputy warned breathlessly. "Avelyn LeStage is one dangerous woman."

"Avelyn?" Cole repeated. "Lisa said her name was Ava."

"The Crowleys simplified the name when they adopted the girls. But they went back to Avelyn when she was committed to a state hospital."

"Committed for what?" he managed.

"Attempted murder, but the foster girl she stabbed lived, so Avelyn eventually got out. Then, poof. She's off the grid someplace—until several people she'd been associated with turned up missing this past year."

And now she's found the girl she blamed for all her problems, he thought darkly.

As he continued climbing, he finally heard the deputy tell Tyler, "Gotcha, buddy. Hold on tight now, and I'll—"

Two sharp cries echoed as a large rock hurtled down,

cracking the fallen tree beneath it before banging its way lower.

"Tyler! Deputy Keller!" Cole shouted, but the only answer was the crashing of the rocks.

Chapter Nineteen

"Why?" Lisa pleaded, not caring if Ava shot her for refusing to get up. "Why do any of this for Sabra? She hurt you, tortured you, worse than she ever did to me."

Ava shook her blue-streaked hair away from her face. "You really don't get it, do you? But then, you never did. None of them did. My sister didn't *torture* me, she *taught* me. And I could've learned so much more, could've taught my sister a few things, too, if you hadn't gone and run your mouth and ruined everything."

"It was Sabra who wrecked things, not me. She murdered Jerry Crowley. For heaven's sake, your sister poisoned you, too."

Ava laughed again, a sound that raised the fine hairs behind Lisa's neck. "Wrong again," she said. "Poisoning was far too subtle for Sabra's tastes. I did it, for her sake. But I gave the rest of us a little taste, too, so the police would never figure out who—"

"You?" Lisa shuddered at the thought. Ava had been only nine then. Nine years old, and already a subtler and more dangerous predator than the sister she admired. "Why? Why would you do that, then hide the poison in her bedroom?"

"We shared a room—don't you remember? Besides, I knew that once people started saying that she'd killed him, no one would ever laugh at her again. And no one would ever mess with me again when I said I was her sister."

Lisa could scarcely believe that the shy girl she'd once pitied was so completely insane.

"But when you told your father, it all went to hell in a hurry. Sabra was dead, Mrs. Crowley lost it and they sent me to a new foster family with a father who made Jerry Crowley look like a freakin' saint. Then, after I turned up pregnant, he dragged me to some clinic and made me get an abortion. Made me kill my flesh and blood so he wouldn't get in trouble."

"You…you were molested?"

"Raped."

"And then he made you get rid of your child?" Lisa found herself beginning to understand how, in a twisted mind like Ava's, the decision to pay her back by killing Tyler made some sick sort of sense.

But Ava wasn't interested in prolonging the discussion.

"Now on your feet," she ordered. "I told you to *move, bitch.*"

Though Ava prodded her painfully with the muzzle of the AK-47, Lisa didn't budge. Why postpone her own death, with Tyler gone already? That would only allow Ava more opportunity to torment her.

Attack her, then. Fight back until she's forced to end things quickly. That way, at least, Cole wouldn't get himself killed in an attempt to save her.

At the thought of the man who'd sacrificed so much and given so wholeheartedly, the pain of regret shafted through her. *I'm so sorry, Cole, so sorry to hurt you this way. Whatever happened that day in Afghanistan, you deserve peace and forgiveness. You deserve…everything.*

Ava's head jerked as she looked toward a sound, a voice, perhaps, that Lisa couldn't quite make out.

More agitated than ever, Ava started kicking Lisa's legs. "Get up. *Now,* or I swear, he'll find your brains splattered right here. But don't worry, I'll give him a moment to shed a tear before I finish him, too."

The thought of Cole falling prey had Lisa springing to her feet. "No!" she cried, hurling herself toward her opponent so swiftly and decisively that she caught Ava still balanced on one foot.

The other woman fell hard onto her back, reflexively squeezing off a shot, but the AK-47's muzzle was pointed sideways and the bullets pinged harmlessly off the nearby rocks. Snarling like an enraged beast, she tried to bring the barrel up, but Lisa was already on her, slamming the insane woman back down.

The impact came at a price, though, giving Ava an opportunity to rake her nails across Lisa's face. Desperate to save her eyes, she jerked back—and that was all the opportunity Ava needed to draw her knees to her chest and kick Lisa off her.

As Cole raced toward the sound of gunfire, agony blasted through his leg with each step, shredding the gauzy curtain between past and present.

And just that quickly, he was once again staggering toward the market in the white-hot desert sunlight. Fighting through pain, carrying a bullet from the ambush that had wounded him and killed another of his fellow Rangers. Not knowing whether the tip about a suicide bomber in the market had been real or just bait to draw his team out, he kept moving, racing the clock, racing his body's impending collapse, throwing himself into an unsecured position and looking down his rifle's barrel through the scope.

And hesitating once more as he sighted a female target

in the crosshair.... A target whose face was silhouetted by the cold glow of the headlights.

His vision blurred, the searing Afghan sun resurfacing to blind him...until the sound of Lisa's pained cry cut through the fatal haze.

"Avelyn!" he shouted, suddenly remembering. "Avelyn LeStage!"

Jerking her head upward, a woman looked his way, her weapon rising to take aim.

And in this time, in this place, Ranger Captain Cole Sawyer pulled the trigger just in time.

"COLE? COLE!" Lisa shouted, stepping carefully around what was left of Ava as she staggered toward him.

He blinked hard, then squinted at her, the shock on his face giving way to relief. Quickly moving forward, he embraced her so tightly she could barely breathe.

"Lisa, you're alive. I thought for sure that one of those shots—"

Sagging in his arms, she sobbed, "Ava killed him! She killed Tyler, and she was—she was going to kill you, too."

"Shh, Lisa. It's going to be all—"

Pulling back, she glared at him. "Don't you *dare* tell me it's going to be all right. Because I can't live through this again. I won't."

"Listen to me," he said sharply. "Tyler is—"

"I don't want to listen. I—I just want to take back these past four days."

"You can never do that," he said, his voice grim. "All you can do is keep fighting until you find the way forward."

Without saying anything more, he started dragging her through the woods, though he was limping heavily.

"No! What are you *doing?*" she shouted, fighting him.

Couldn't he see that she only wanted to lie down and die herself?

"What am I doing? I'm trying to tell you that Tyler needs you and I'm taking you to him."

"Tyler? He's alive?" Weakened by shock, her knees buckled. "And you—you left him somewhere out here with his throat cut? What were you *thinking?*"

"I was thinking of saving your life. And I don't know what Ava told you, but nobody cut Tyler's throat."

Ava had lied about killing Tyler? The thought spun dizzily through Lisa's throbbing head. Of course the woman had lied, inflicting one final dose of her cruel venom.

With that realization, fresh strength surged through Lisa's body, strength borne of the hope that had kept her going for the past four days. She was going to see Tyler. Going to hold her son in her arms again.

"But he's still in danger," Cole was saying. "So—"

Whatever else he said was lost as she rushed past him, until he suddenly pulled her up short in front of what she realized was a long split in the earth.

"Careful," he said. "That first step is a killer." Turning toward the void, he shouted, "Tyler? Deputy? I've got someone up here who's just dying to—"

"How 'bout a hand here, Sawyer?" a gruff female voice called from the ravine. "If you can reach down and grab him, I've almost got him up."

"Tyler!" Lisa shouted, tears springing to her eyes as she surged past, threw herself down on her stomach and reached over the edge.

"Mommy!" her son cried, and even in the dark, she could make him out as he struggled to reach her arms.

She inched forward, desperate to touch, to hold, to love forever, the son she and Cole had come so far and suffered so much to rescue.

"I've got you, Lisa," Cole said as he grabbed her belt and held fast, giving her the strength and surety she needed to finally grasp the small arms and lift the tiny boy from the abyss.

"Mommy!" Tyler cried, submitting to her kisses and hugging her while Cole helped the other woman to safety. "Deputy Keller says she has a whole drawer full of junior deputy badges—and she promised she's going to give me *five!*"

Chapter Twenty

Sweating and exhausted, Deputy Trace Sutherland was relieved when the physical therapist finally told him it was time to go back to his room.

Still, he forced himself to ask, "Are you sure? I think I could do a little more."

The toned, dark-skinned woman smiled at him, the silvery threads in her close-cropped hair the only hint of her age. "You're gonna walk again, Trace Sutherland, and soon. I can always tell."

Though he hurt in places he'd been unable to feel two days before, he managed to grin back. "Walking? Nothing doing. I'm taking you out dancing this New Year's Eve."

She laughed at that and said, "Let's get you back to your room before you put me in a diabetic coma with all that sugar of yours."

As she wheeled him down the hall, the voices floating out from his room sounded anything but sweet.

"I've told you more than once, Jill Keller, you're not welcome here."

Trace grimaced to hear his mother talking to Jill that way.

"I'm sorry you feel that way, Mrs. Sutherland, but I'm not leaving. Not until Trace tells me himself that he doesn't want me in his life." Abruptly, Jill's anger gave way to the streak of sassiness he'd always found so sexy. "It's not like he doesn't have experience."

"Sounds a little intense in there," the physical therapist whispered. "Want me to wheel you back to PT till this blows over?"

Trace shook his head. "I'd better settle this before the fur starts flying."

"Knock, knock," the woman sang before she wheeled him through the door.

Both women turned toward him, and in Jill's eyes he saw something softer and far more vulnerable than he'd ever seen there before. Even after the miscarriage, she'd been so quick to strap on her armor, to vent her fury at the man who'd been jailed for beating her so savagely, that he had only caught rare, sidelong glimpses of her pain.

But the moment she spotted him, something cracked wide open, and, without even waiting for the physical therapist to help him back into bed, she went to her knees beside his chair, taking his hand and pressing her face to it.

"Forgive me," she begged, voice breaking. "Please forgive me, Trace."

As the physical therapist quietly withdrew, Trace shook his head in confusion, feeling Jill's tears dampening his skin—the first tears he had witnessed in all the years he'd known her. "For what? Surely, you can't think— You couldn't have possibly known there'd be an accident."

"I don't mean just the accident. I'm talking about how I always kept you at a distance, how I pushed you away after our baby... My priorities were so far out of line. My stubbornness, my pride..."

"I knew it was all her fault." Nodding sagely, his mother crossed her arms over her ample bosom. "The accident, the marriage. I told her you wouldn't want her here, sapping your energy and delaying your recov—"

"Mom," he interrupted, "I love you very much, and I'm glad you're here for me. But right now I need to be alone with my wife."

"Sweetie, you're still confused. Jill's your ex-wife. Remember?"

"That's where you're wrong," he told her, "because if I have anything to say about it, Jill and I aren't finished. Not by a long shot. Now please, will you excuse us?"

Sighing loudly, his mother shook her head and said, "If that's what you really want..." as she walked out the door.

Once they were alone, he lifted Jill's hand to his lips and kissed it. "Jill? Jill, look at me, please."

She looked up into his face, her blue eyes reddened and her lashes clumped with moisture.

Wiping away her tears, he said, "Never, ever apologize to me for who you are. I fell in love with you because you're opinionated, gutsy as hell, exciting—the polar opposite of me."

"I wouldn't exactly say you're not exciting...." she murmured, the wicked spark in her eyes reminding him of times the two of them had been alone and out of uniform.

"I love you because you're you," he said, "and I was wrong, very wrong, to try to change you with some stupid ultimatum about your job."

"Maybe," she whispered, "but do you think we might be able to find some middle ground?"

"I know we will," he said, pulling her into his arms and kissing the woman he had vowed to love for all his life.

LIGHT AGAIN, A brilliant glare that made Cole's head hurt when he first cracked open his eyes. Raising his hand to cover them, he felt a pinch in his arm.

"Careful. You'll pull out your IV," a female voice said.

A voice he would know anywhere, though it was thickened with emotion.

"Lisa," he managed, his throat so parched the words came out a hoarse rasp. "What? Where are…?"

"I'm furious with you, Cole Sawyer."

He blinked, squinting in complete confusion at the fuzzy image of her scowl. "How did I get—"

"You passed out the moment you got Jill Keller out of that ravine. Scared the devil out of me. And when I finally saw how much blood you'd lost…" Her face loomed over his, its beauty coming into focus as she squeezed his hand. "I was afraid I'd never get the chance to tell you how much everything you've done has meant, and how I feel about—"

"Where's Tyler?"

A warm smile misted her eyes. "Fast asleep at the hotel, with his octopus in his arms and my dad sitting right beside him. The doctors checked him out and released him yesterday. He's going to be okay—thanks to you and Jill Keller."

"Your father's here? How did he get— Where are we?"

"You were taken to Alpine, to the nearest hospital," she explained. "Things didn't look good by the time you got here, but they gave you a transfusion to get you stabilized."

"How long ago?" he asked, noticing she was wearing a white blouse and a pair of jeans he hadn't seen before. Other than a few scratches on her face, she looked unharmed.

"I'm sorry, Cole. That was yesterday morning, and you had surgery earlier today to remove the bullet from your leg. It's going to be fine, but…you missed your meeting in Georgia."

"It's not important," he said, knowing that between the

investigation into the events of the past few days and his injury, his chances of becoming a U.S. Marshal any time soon had gone down the drain. "You and Tyler are safe, and that's all that matters."

A debt repaid to a man he had once failed. Yet somehow he had screwed up again, allowing himself to fall in love with Lisa. Allowing himself, a man without a future, to imagine taking Devin Meador's place beside his wife.

"What about you?" he asked. "Are you feeling better?"

"I'll need to take it easy for a few weeks," she said, gingerly touching her head, "but I'm going to be just fine. Except I've wanted so badly to tell you how very much I..."

When words failed her, she showed him instead, bending to press her lips to his mouth, softly, gently, until living sparks beneath his skin caught fire. Before he could stop himself, he slid his hand along her forearm, reveling in the sensation of her smooth flesh beneath his calloused fingers. The fact that she was kissing him at all, that she could accept what he had told her about that day in Lashkar Gah—accept *him*—inflamed him further. He pulled her even closer, his desperation growing with the knowledge that, for the sake of honor, he was kissing her goodbye.

Just one more minute and I'll let her go. I'll let her go forever. But one minute tumbled into the next, and the hand that grazed her sweet breast stopped to linger, his fingers toying with the budding nipple, his excitement swelling at her soft moan. When he reached to unfasten the front clasp of her bra for better access, she finally pulled away.

"Better slow down, Cole," she whispered, sounding breathless, "or we'll pull out those stitches for sure."

"I—I'm sorry," he said. His skin was burning and his body—a body that cared nothing for either decency or honor—was aching to reach for her, to claim her for his own. "I shouldn't— I have no right—"

"I want you to know," she said, "I care about you, too. I had no idea how much until I saw you lying there, so pale and—I was terrified that I would lose you, too. Like Devin."

"Don't you remember what I said about your husband?" he asked carefully. "About being there that day when…"

"You nearly died to save my son, Cole Sawyer. You nearly died to save my life. Whatever happened in Afghanistan, whatever you insist on blaming yourself for, I won't believe it was your fault. Were *you* the one who strapped an explosive harness on your body? The one who found that crowded market my husband was patrolling and—"

"Of course not, but I should have—"

"If it's forgiveness you need, you've more than earned mine, Cole," she said quietly. "You deserve—we both deserve—the chance to move forward. Please."

"What are you saying?"

"I'm saying that I know it's probably too soon, and maybe I'll scare you off, but after everything I've been through, I don't want to waste one more day of my life being frightened. I want to wrap my hands around this chance and—" She laughed softly, clearly at herself, then looked at him through lowered lashes. "I'm trying to tell you that what I feel for you goes so much deeper than gratitude. I love you, Cole. I truly love you, and I want… I want more than anything to have you in my life—mine and my son's."

As a blush darkened her cheeks, he let her words sink in, the unimaginable gift of them. Just one of many gifts she'd given him these past few days. But as badly as he wanted to tell her that he, too, had fallen in love, he couldn't break free of the past's hold—or his concerns about his future.

So instead he said, "It's been a tough time, Lisa. A really emotional time for everyone involved. How 'bout we let this thing cool off for a while? Until we can both be certain and I have a—"

"I'm certain," she said, without an instant's hesitation. But already she was pulling back, her brown eyes shuttering, telling him that his clumsy attempt to allow her a graceful way out had instead hurt her deeply. "But maybe you're right. In the heat of the moment people say things, like you did the other night in the car, after we—"

"Lisa," he tried, grappling for some way to make her understand.

But she was already backing toward the door, her head shaking. "It's all right. You don't have to explain. I understand that you're a bachelor, with no strings to hold you. Why would you want to tie yourself down to a woman with so much baggage?"

"Lisa, please. That's not it." But it was too late. Turning away, she rushed through the door, and when he tried to follow, a brutal stab of pain from his fresh incision knocked him back to the pillows.

Which gave him plenty of time to consider the real reason he remained unattached at the age of thirty-one. A reason that had far less to do with his military service than it did with his knack for tripping over his tongue and saying the wrong thing.

Six weeks later...

"AND THEY ALL LIVED HAPPILY ever after," Lisa whispered, finishing the story for her own sake, though Tyler and the softly snoring Rowdy were both conked out after hours of raucous play.

Leaning forward to kiss the soft curve of her son's cheek and smooth his tangled blankets, she reminded herself that this was the happily ever after she had prayed for during those dark nights in October. Nights in which she'd sworn that if Tyler were returned to her safely, she would never ask for anything again.

Would never dream of another fairy tale, especially not with a man she'd known from the start planned to leave town. A man who hadn't even let her know where he was going.

Her heart ached with the memory of showing up at the home he had been renting and finding it had been vacated. But after she had so foolishly turned her back and walked out on him, avoiding him during all the days of questioning that took place before authorities had officially cleared them both, what had she expected?

It was for the best, she told herself as she headed downstairs, where her father was waiting to help her finish decorating the tree they had all picked out earlier. Between work and the more important job of raising her son, it wasn't as if she had room in her life to build a future with a man who couldn't put the past behind him.

Downstairs, she heard voices from the den and realized her father had abandoned his post to catch yet another football game. Smiling at his weakness for the sport, she shook her head, went over to the abandoned tree and began to hang the shiny red bulbs—a new set she had bought, vowing to build new memories—reminding herself to count her blessings with each one.

When she finished, she picked up the gaudy, glittering star Tyler had chosen and looked around for a chair so she could reach the top of the tree. But then the pocket door between the living room and the den slid open, and a tall man stepped into the room, the very man whose face she had been fighting so hard to banish from her dreams.

"Cole?"

"Don't you screw this up again, boy," her father called, grinning. Shifting his gaze to her, he added, "And you, sweetheart, this time you sit still and actually *listen* so I don't have to suffer through your moping over the holidays."

"Moping?" she asked, wanting to deny it, but her father merely shook his head as Cole slid the door closed. Looking at him, she said, "I wasn't moping."

"I was," he admitted with a sheepish smile. "*And* I've been biting guys' heads off at my new job."

"You have a new job?" she asked, nervously fiddling with the star, her heart pounding.

"I do," he said with a smile. "Turns out my old C.O. recommended me for a special critical response team. It's a civilian law enforcement position that serves smaller communities throughout the state. They needed a good marksman to help save lives in hostage situations when negotiations break down and there's no other option.

"After what happened in Lashkar Gah, I didn't think I could ever do that work again," he said, "but what we went through together reminded me that I can make a positive difference, a crucial difference, under stressful circumstances."

"You made all the difference in the world for Tyler and me," she said honestly. "If you can do that for other families, it's wonderful, Cole, the greatest gift I can imagine. So, why are you biting people's heads off and standing here looking so serious?"

"Because I'm so damned nervous." His clear gray eyes

locked with hers. "Scared to death I'll say the wrong thing again, and this time I'll lose you forever."

"Lose me?" She shook her head. "But I thought you didn't want me."

"No, Lisa. God help me, that was never it at all. Far from it. I *do* want you, you and your son—all three of us together. But I couldn't… Your forgiveness was one thing, a huge thing, but it never would have worked until I found some way to make peace with myself."

"So have you, Cole?"

"I was shot that day in Afghanistan, too," he said. "Ambushed on the way to respond. One of my men was killed and another critically injured, but I kept going, pushing. Until I saw the woman's face in my scope. Saw the desperation in it."

"She knew she was about to die."

"Yes, and for just an instant I *felt* instead of acted—but I wasn't there to empathize, or to wonder if she was being forced, and because I let myself wonder, that single second was enough to give her the chance to set off the bomb."

"You were injured. You were human," she said, compassion welling up inside her. "And you've proven since then that you're more than capable of—"

"I just needed you to understood. To know all of it, before I could—" Taking the star from her, he set it down carefully on a lamp table before pulling her into his arms. "I'm finished living in the past, Lisa. And there's no future that would make me happier than one that has you in it. I love you," he said into her ear, his warm breath sending a delicious ripple through her body. "And I want nothing more than the chance to spend all the days and years of my life getting to know you even better. If you'll only give me the chance to—"

"I'll give you more than a chance," she said. "I'll give you everything, Cole."

And then their lips met in a kiss that bound their fates and sealed their future. A kiss that vanquished bitter memories and helped them chart a path to forging new ones....

And at some point, hours later, allowed them to place a star together on the yuletide tree.

* * * * *

REQUEST YOUR FREE BOOKS!
2 FREE NOVELS PLUS 2 FREE GIFTS!

◆ Harlequin®

INTRIGUE®

BREATHTAKING ROMANTIC SUSPENSE

YES! Please send me 2 FREE Harlequin Intrigue® novels and my 2 FREE gifts (gifts are worth about $10). After receiving them, if I don't wish to receive any more books, I can return the shipping statement marked "cancel." If I don't cancel, I will receive 6 brand-new novels every month and be billed just $4.49 per book in the U.S. or $5.24 per book in Canada. That's a saving of at least 14% off the cover price! It's quite a bargain! Shipping and handling is just 50¢ per book in the U.S. and 75¢ per book in Canada.* I understand that accepting the 2 free books and gifts places me under no obligation to buy anything. I can always return a shipment and cancel at any time. Even if I never buy another book, the two free books and gifts are mine to keep forever.

182/382 HDN FEQ2

Name	(PLEASE PRINT)	
Address		Apt. #
City	State/Prov.	Zip/Postal Code

Signature (if under 18, a parent or guardian must sign)

Mail to the **Reader Service:**
IN U.S.A.: P.O. Box 1867, Buffalo, NY 14240-1867
IN CANADA: P.O. Box 609, Fort Erie, Ontario L2A 5X3

Not valid for current subscribers to Harlequin Intrigue books.

**Are you a subscriber to Harlequin Intrigue books
and want to receive the larger-print edition?
Call 1-800-873-8635 or visit www.ReaderService.com.**

* Terms and prices subject to change without notice. Prices do not include applicable taxes. Sales tax applicable in N.Y. Canadian residents will be charged applicable taxes. Offer not valid in Quebec. This offer is limited to one order per household. All orders subject to credit approval. Credit or debit balances in a customer's account(s) may be offset by any other outstanding balance owed by or to the customer. Please allow 4 to 6 weeks for delivery. Offer available while quantities last.

Your Privacy—The Reader Service is committed to protecting your privacy. Our Privacy Policy is available online at www.ReaderService.com or upon request from the Reader Service.

We make a portion of our mailing list available to reputable third parties that offer products we believe may interest you. If you prefer that we not exchange your name with third parties, or if you wish to clarify or modify your communication preferences, please visit us at www.ReaderService.com/consumerchoice or write to us at Reader Service Preference Service, P.O. Box 9062, Buffalo, NY 14269. Include your complete name and address.

HI11B

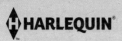

Read on for a sneak peak of
JUSTICE AT CARDWELL RANCH,
the highly anticipated sequel to
CRIME SCENE AT CARWELL RANCH,
read by over 2 million readers,
by USA TODAY *bestselling author B.J. Daniels!*

Out of the corner of her eye, she saw that the SUV was empty. Past it, near the trailhead, she glimpsed the beam of a flashlight bobbing as it headed down the trail.

The trail was wide and paved, and she found, once her eyes adjusted, that she didn't need to use her flashlight if she was careful. Enough starlight bled down through the pine boughs that she could see far enough ahead—she also knew the trail well.

There was no sign of Jordan, though. She'd reached the creek and bridge, quickly crossed it, and had started up the winding trail when she caught a glimpse of light above her on the trail.

She stopped to listen, afraid he might have heard her behind him. But there was only the sound of the creek and moan of the pines in the breeze. Somewhere in the distance, an owl hooted. She moved again, hurrying now.

Once the trail topped out, she should be able to see Jordan's light ahead of her, though she couldn't imagine what he was doing hiking to the falls tonight.

There was always a good chance of running into a moose or a wolf or, worse, this time of a year, a hungry grizzly foraging for food before hibernation.

The trail topped out. She stopped to catch her breath and listen for Jordan. Ahead she could make out the solid rock area at the base of the falls. A few more steps and she could feel the mist coming off the cascading water. From here, the trail carved a crooked path up through the pines to the top of the falls.

There was no sign of any light ahead and the only thing she could hear was the falls. Where was Jordan? She rushed on, convinced he was still ahead of her. Something rustled in the trees off to her right. A limb cracked somewhere ahead in the pines.

She stopped and drew her weapon. Someone was out there.

The report of the rifle shot felt so close it made the hair stand up on her neck. The sound ricocheted off the rock cliff and reverberated through her. Liza dived to the ground. A second shot echoed through the trees.

Weapon still drawn, she scrambled up the hill and almost tripped over the body Jordan Cardwell was standing over.

What was Jordan doing up at the falls so late at night? And is he guilty of more than just a walk in the moonlight?

Find out in the highly anticipated sequel
JUSTICE AT CARWELL RANCH
by USA TODAY *bestselling author*
B.J. Daniels.

Catch the thrill October 2, 2012.

SPECIAL EDITION

Life, Love and Family

Sometimes love strikes in the most unexpected circumstances...

Soon-to-be single mom Antonia Wright isn't looking for romance, especially from a cowboy. But when rancher and single father Clayton Traub rents a room at Antonia's boardinghouse, Wright's Way, she isn't prepared for the attraction that instantly sizzles between them or the pain she sees in his big brown eyes. Can Clay and Antonia trust their hearts and build the family they've always dreamed of?

Don't miss

THE MAVERICK'S READY-MADE FAMILY

by Brenda Harlen

Available this October from Harlequin® Special Edition®

www.Harlequin.com

HSE65697

HARLEQUIN® *Blaze*™

red-hot reads

Two sizzling fairy tales with men straight from your wildest dreams...

Fan-favorite authors

Rhonda Nelson & Karen Foley

bring readers another installment of

Blazing Bedtime Stories, Volume IX

THE EQUALIZER

Modern-day righter of wrongs, Robin Sherwood is a man on a mission and will do everything necessary to see that through, especially when that means catching the eye of a fair maiden.

GOD'S GIFT TO WOMEN

Sculptor Lexi Adams decides there is no such thing as the perfect man, until she catches sight of Nikos Christakos, the sexy builder next door. She convinces herself that she only wants to sculpt him, but soon finds a cold stone statue is a poor substitute for the real deal.

Available October 2012 wherever books are sold.

HARLEQUIN® Romance

At their grandmother's request, three estranged
sisters return home for Christmas to the small town
of Beckett's Run. Little do they know that this family
reunion will reveal long-buried secrets...
and new-found love.

Discover the magic of Christmas in a brand-new
Harlequin® Romance miniseries.

Holiday Miracles

In October 2012, find yourself
SNOWBOUND IN THE EARL'S CASTLE
by **Fiona Harper**

Be enchanted in November 2012 by a
SLEIGH RIDE WITH THE RANCHER
by **Donna Alward**

And be mesmerized in December 2012 by
MISTLETOE KISSES WITH THE BILLIONAIRE
by **Shirley Jump**

Available wherever books are sold.